Anonymous

Macalpine; Or, on Scottish Ground

A Novel: Vol. II

Anonymous

Macalpine; Or, on Scottish Ground
A Novel: Vol. II

ISBN/EAN: 9783337056575

Printed in Europe, USA, Canada, Australia, Japan

Cover: Foto ©Andreas Hilbeck / pixelio.de

More available books at **www.hansebooks.com**

MACALPINE;

OR,

ON SCOTTISH GROUND.

PRINTED BY BALLANTYNE AND COMPANY
EDINBURGH AND LONDON

MACALPINE;

OR,

ON SCOTTISH GROUND.

𝔄 𝔑𝔬𝔳𝔢𝔩.

"Who aspires
To genuine greatness
Temper with the sternness of the brain
Thoughts motherly and meek as womanhood.
Books, leisure, perfect freedom, and the talk
Man holds with week-day man:
These are the degrees
By which true sway doth mount."
—WORDSWORTH.

VOL. II.

LONDON:
SAMPSON LOW, MARSTON, LOW, & SEARLE,
CROWN BUILDINGS, 188 FLEET STREET.
1872.

MACALPINE;

OR,

ON SCOTTISH GROUND.

———◇———

CHAPTER XV.

UPON Ellen's return to Edinburgh, goaded by her old little world's rejection of her in her fallen fortunes, her mind dwelt upon the mystery which had enveloped the conduct of her parents. The subject had hitherto been sacredly hid in her own breast, and was little brought up even there.

The flowers that grow over the tomb are sacredly touched; the spirit awakes the memories of those who lie beneath with a tenderness which is the due of their eternal close with life. But be these assailed by others ignorant of their virtue or their redeeming lights, the

VOL. II.   A

delicate regard becomes troubled. It is not always it can repel with indignant scorn : to few is given the power to defy the world's round judgments which have behind them the stern moral laws ; it is by more than human strength, the ability to stand forward to the question, How are these to be thrust aside for thee? Ellen was now cast back upon herself, and in that contact with the raw world which excites the mind into a sharp dealing with every care.

Reginald Lee and his wife, for all Ellen could learn, came to the town of Tarbet as if from the clouds. He took a modest house comparatively with others around, even in that modest little town ; and on its door-plate was engraved, "Mr Lee, surgeon." Beyond that announcement nothing more was known of the couple. The surgeon had demands made upon his professional skill by the poor, who take the benefactions of the doctor as a right. For a year or two Mr Lee was regarded by the wealthier inhabitants askance. But patience, combined with real talent, though quiet and undemonstrative, especially if possessed by a man whose appearance and manner indicate elevation of character, will in time command attention ; and Mr Lee, in the course of two or three years, was approved of by some of the "best people" of the town. He came out more, though still maintaining some distance and reserve, and his practice became large and remunerative. There seemed, however, something, the gossips said, upon the mind of himself and his wife. The inhabitants of Tarbet were curious to know the history of the spouses, of whom little or nothing was known. Mr Lee had been an army surgeon, and had been abroad : thus much he told in reply to the most adventurous querists, and even spoke now and again of numerous incidents in his travel in foreign lands. They were visited by nobody but patients ; and whether Scotch, English, Irish, or of foreign birth, might not have been known, save that the dialect of Mrs Lee indicated that she at least belonged to the country in which she now lived.

Mrs Lee brought an infant daughter with her to Tarbet, and she never had another child. After six years they removed to a house of some pretensions, and things prospered well with them.

But a blow came to this prosperity. The other medical men of the town, and others who bark at every success, had got hold of some vague information from a person on a visit from India, professing to have known something of Mr Lee; and they fanned the old embers of mystery which surrounded him into a fierce flame,—turning, to commonplace people, a fast dying-out suspicion into a blatant horror. The doctor was doomed; his practice again became confined to the humbler classes. It was fortunate for him and his companion that they were independent of society. Placing them under the ban only contributed to lessen the

income of the surgeon—never served to affect
their happiness.   Much of this Mr Lee found
in his work, and the rest in his books, and the
society of her he loved without diminution
throughout the course of his days.

Young Ellen soon grew up able to give him
an additional happiness.   Even in the few companions of her girlhood (introduced into the
house with infantile awe) her parents might
have met with amusement : Mrs Lee did, not
so her husband.   His temper could not brook
prattle where he was denied cultivated society.
The doctor was a Conservative of a particular
type : all his people were to him only patients,
not friends with whom he sat on terms of
equality ; although kind and just in his attitude to them, they were inferior beings with
whom he had no feeling in common.   A proud,
stiff, but not soulless man : Ellen Lee never
knew a father's true love.

Dr Lee's death was followed a few years
afterwards by that of his wife.   Two persons

alone were known to Ellen as friends of her
parents, to whom she might look for assistance
in the situation in which she was placed :
these were Oliver Arnot and Mrs Macbean.
The former had paid a visit to Mrs Lee soon
after her husband's death, and Ellen understood him to be her uncle. The latter, as we
have seen, she had known from her own childhood.

The retired life of her parents seemed
strange in Ellen's eyes as soon as her existence
out of doors was sufficiently advanced to in-
form her of the conduct and feelings of others,
and appreciate the wounds she did not fail to
receive from vulgar minds. But any youthful
spirit of inquiry was checked by her mother ;
while, as she grew up, and education and reading further refined the delicacy of her spirit, the
subject became painful to her, and she thought
it best to let it alone. And indeed, after all,
the gravity of her fears might have been the reaction from her own sometimes over-lively fancy.

"Martha," said Ellen to her companion one evening over the fire, as autumn was making itself felt coldly in the grey capital, "I wish my father and mother had been like other people."

"And were they not like other people, and better too?" said Mrs Macbean, startled by Ellen's abrupt speech. "No more accomplished or truer gentleman than Dr Lee lived in the land; as for your mother, there was no beauty and sense to match hers. I'm thinking they were too good for the puir folks of Tarbet."

"Isolation from the world generally brings sorrow," said Ellen; "if it had not been for you, dear Martha, I would have been alive without a friend. I reflect with joy upon my parents' love; it will last as the first, brightest, and purest in all my memories. But there is always a sadness connected with it : it is not the healthy joy with which I think over my days at Finzean. There is an ineffaceable sorrow lying upon my recollections of home."

" Ah, that is because your good father and
mother are dead, while the hero of Finzean
lives before you."

" No, dear Martha, it 's not that," replied
Ellen, putting her arm round the old lady's
neck, and looking into her face with thought-
ful sadness. " Though so devoted to each
other, there was a constraint in their lives,—
even with themselves, though they stole away
from others to remain alone bound up in each
other. Several times I found my mother in tears,
without any apparent cause; and when I con-
doled with her on my father's loss of practice,
I always thought there was a deeper cause
which she hid away in her bosom. Generous,
open-hearted mother! there was that too sacred
in the recesses of thy breast for even an only
child to know."

When Mrs Macbean looked at Ellen by the
gleam of the rising fire, the tears were stream-
ing from her eyes. The old lady was restless
and uneasy. Ellen had been reading poetry

recently, and her style of speech was, in her sensitiveness, influenced thereby, as were her thoughts also.

"Ellen, my love, you are ill," Mrs Macbean said; "you vex yourself with matters now dead and gone; and your mother's sorrow should be forgotten for ever."

"It was certainly not unkindness to each other which preyed upon their spirits," she added, quietly, in a tone by which it might be understood the subject was dropped.

"No," said Ellen, regaining her composure, "they were more like lovers of a month, than husband and wife of years' standing,—that is to say, if marriage is truly said to dull the inspiration of the presence of those we love. I have seen my father in the moonlight, under the shadow of the ruins of the monastery which bordered our house, charm my mother with an air on the lute, while she would throw up the window and reply by a verse from a Scottish ballad, in the sweet plaintive voice

which has often delighted us; and he would
play the part of 'Romeo' to her 'Juliet,'
where, at the balcony, the tale is told of their
love. She would tell me afterwards the story
of the play, and warn me, with much fervour,
against rash love. Do you not think, Martha,
that my mother's grief came of some such
romance?"

"The subject is painful to you, my girl,"
said Mrs Macbean, "as it is to me. You must
forget it."

"No, Martha, it affects my own life. Think
you I can remain quiet with some mysterious
fate hanging over me," said Ellen, aroused by
her friend's almost admitted knowledge.

"Surely," Mrs Macbean said, suddenly,
"this does not in any way account for your
conduct to Alan Macalpine."

"It does not," replied Ellen; "but if I had
no other reason for not acceding to his suit,
that one might perhaps be enough, that I am
not sure I am what I am told I am."

"You will have to go to India if you wish to know your mother's history there," said Mrs Macbean, quietly.

"Not so far, Martha, if those who knew my mother best in this country would speak," answered Ellen, in a persuasive manner. Mrs Macbean turned her looks off the bold flame that now and again lit up Ellen's animated but pale countenance. "I will be open with you, Martha, and tell you what I do know. A day before my mother's death she gave me the key of her private cabinet, and, looking for a packet which was sealed, that she might destroy it with her own hand, I opened a Bible which I had never seen ; a name was written on the fly leaf which had been blotted out, but I could see it was neither that of Arnot nor Lee."

"Do you doubt your own mother, Ellen," asked Mrs Macbean, quickly.

"No doubt—but what is it ? You may set my mind at rest. You were her confidant, Martha;

her long, perhaps only friend ; and are you not mine—Aunt Martha, as I was taught to call you ? You should know the secret, if secret there be ; tell me it. What untold crimes could so gentle a being have committed that it seems dreadful to you to tell the truth ?" The speaker rose from her seat, astonished alike at her own force, but looking on her companion, who hid her face away in pain.

"No one," muttered Mrs Macbean, alarmed and offended, "is calling her innocence or her honour in question."

"Yes they are—the whole world is—all the world to me. Does not my uncle dread that I should arise from my obscurity, that I should unite my life with any one but an easy unenquiring being like himself. Do not the people of Tarbet hold away their looks from the poor victim of her birth, because the name of her mother is questioned."

"Stay, Ellen," cried Mrs Macbean, rising from her seat, afraid at the determined manner of Ellen, and dreading her power to resist her inquiries further.

"Martha," Ellen cried, as she heard Mrs Macbean passing out; but the old lady was gone.

The conduct of Mrs Macbean more than confirmed Ellen's fears. Her position she was now assured was equivocal—which might require that she should seek a home in some new land, and form a history for herself.

Yet she was not cast down. She worked on, cheerful as she could, advancing in her knowledge of books and the world, and utterly refusing to give way to the shock. Her life had taught her differently than vainly regretting. Chiefly of him from whom she had parted, she had learned some love and faith concerning humanity and its world, however much she felt for the present that a stern hand was upon her. Severed for ever, to all appearance, from him she loved—alone in the world —tainted in the estimation of the acquaintances of her past life—and now also suffering from a wounded spirit in the service by which she earned her bread,—if she came through the ordeal without being crushed, she might well thank God for it. One effect of the increased activity of her emotions was to make her more exacting in estimating the moral qualities demanded in intercourse with others —a state of mind for which some heroism is necessary. To be affable with all—the embodiments of vice as virtue—conduces most to the peace and comfort of common humanity. But fortunately men and women exist who have the courage to disagree with wrong, at the expense of a reputation for amiability, or even of their bread.

The ignorant pair whose children Ellen had hoped to do good to now saw in her pay only an incumbrance, because in her pronounced sense they felt a rebuke of their own incompetency, and they waited only for an opportunity to send her away. Ellen was naturally

too gentle and sensible to offend by any over-
zeal in thinking to approach the minds of the
parents as well as the children, and she suffered
more indignities to herself to pass unobserved
than do generally women of less capacity.
Only the master of the house found his pompous nothings and some pernicious doctrines
very quietly answered now and again at his
dinner-table, when Ellen's independent judgment refused to hide itself. And so Ellen was
fain again to think of other employment. It
had been hard getting this poor affair, which
it appeared would have to be relinquished.
It might be impossible to get one better or
even inferior of the same order of employment,
and what else was there for her in this nine-
teenth century !

Imagine the appearance of Ellen in the
clear, buoyant air of new Edinburgh. Her face
still possessed that hue of health which lies not
in the high complexion of the cheek; yet the
rose was richly tinted to which it naturally

might compare.   The auburn hair gave luxuri-
ance to the head, of the fine oval shape :
and her steady eye, while pensive, had the
scarce latent sparkle of humour.   Her person,
formed for ease and grace, was attired in
simplicity, but with elegance and completeness
which indicated no demand upon the resources
of art.   Her step was on the borders of command, but suggesting rather a lively independence.   Even at a distance, the lithe, neat
figure in its sustained movement possessed a
charm for the admirers of the graceful.

There must exist an inherent nobility of
character above all externals, where this dignity
is preserved over the blighting hands of misfortune.

Ellen attracted little attention beyond that
of the idle pedestrian.   She had not much
society, and what she had, estimated her not
by her true merits.   In the circle of Mistress
· Martha she was appreciated as frank and
kindly, while the small number of unmarried

males saw in the friend of the old lady something beyond that, which they did not understand, and therefore did not care for. There was to their tameness a troublesome superiority which made itself felt, though not expressed, and they had no thoughts of Ellen for a wife. Occasionally she met the young men of the world at the house of the civic dignitary, her employer; but the sons of mammon had nothing to know in the humble daughter of obscurity, whose expression too was rather of hopeful intelligence than voluptuous fire. It is to the easy-minded children of plenty, whose features may be gay with animal health and the eye bright in the sun, who are supported to the full with the dower that decks and feeds, and sets them far away off the eager gnaws of want, that the sons of the day are looking. Heroism and sorrow of the brave, in their bright loneliness, are distasteful, and become subject of reproach.

The civic family was quite equal to appre-

7

ciating what they called the gentility of Ellen, and she was not therefore excluded, but occasionally paraded, before company whom the landlord looked upon as caring for good breeding and " leeterary " talk.

Late in the year, the house was thrown into unusual commotion by the fact that a " Sir " was to dine in it that afternoon. The dignitary was from the Morven way besides, and Ellen was called into requisition, rising for the hour in the estimation of the whole household. The " Sir " had bought an expensive piece of jewellery from the landlord, and the latter, knowing his man, had ventured, upon the strength of their mutual experience of civic business, to invite the purchaser to his house. It was Sir Andrew Cameron, who was always ready to save himself the expense of a dinner ; and in this advanced age he could afford to dine with a shopkeeper who was also a magistrate.

When Sir Andrew entered the dining-room,

it was with the air of importance and condescension he assumed among inferiors. He
spoke loud, stared about him, and seemed to
estimate the cost of the furniture and plenish-
ing. He was at once busy with eye-glass,
pocket-handkerchief, and toothpick, roughly
criticising pictures, hinting at the prices of
things, asking Mrs Jenkins about her family,
with a puffy quickness which indicated his
indifference for the answer, and the very partial respect he had for a man whose means
were comparatively small to his own. He was
assisted largely to the viands ; while he dis-
cussed the topics of the day, and conspicuously
the money-market, with the host, with volu-
bility and unconcern for the other's views, Mr
and Mrs Jenkins worshipped. Sir Andrew
Cameron was a great man, and it behoved
them to treat him as such ; to listen and
answer with awe and respect. To Ellen, on
the other hand, who had never been in the
company of one of the world's great men, Sir

Andrew Cameron's presence was not agreeable.
Dr Lee and Alan Macalpine were the only two
men whose characters responded in her imagination to the call demanded from her life in
the world of books in which she was now
dwelling. The repast went on, and Sir Andrew
rattled away, having all to himself; Ellen having no opportunity of breathing a monosyllable
out of a sense of duty to the house, which was
dumbly oppressed by the heavy honour which
had been laid upon it.

The voice of the landlord was heard in a
lull, intimating that he too was a Tory in
politics. His guest looked as if he was not
the least honoured by the connection.

"You will have no opponents in your quarter, I'm thinking," said the Tory magistrate,
not offended by the other's snub.

"Yes, we have lots," cried Sir Andrew.
"The farmers are going to the devil with
pride. They are throwing off their natural
protectors, and falling in with the agitators;

and our smaller fry are standing upon rights as if they were born with privileges like peers."

Now this speech did irritate Ellen. Somehow she felt a direct thrust in the side of Oliver Arnot and Alan Macalpine, and her heart beat at the impulse of becoming their champion.

"Do you not think, Sir Andrew, that these poor men also have rights," asked Ellen, quietly, while the knight, before he could look at her, felt an unpleasant flush rising into his cheek. It could not possibly be that this obscurity was "taking him off." He looked at her, and became assured she was not.

"No," bawled Sir Andrew, angrily, as the Jenkins family trembled. This was enough to say, according to his usual manner. But there was a something higher in the woman who had addressed him, he somehow felt, which must be taken down. He went on. "They have no rights; if they attend to the work they have, they will have enough to think of."

"They are poor, many of them wretched, and they wish to better their condition in life," answered Ellen. "It is natural, surely."

Sir Andrew changed the conversation at once, but his vanity was wounded by the quiet self-assured manner of the young woman opposite, who had spoken words as if in superiority of his, and he recurred to it again. "Where have you seen this wretchedness, for which you have so much compassion?" he inquired.

"At Morven."

"Where?" he cried.

"At Morven," she repeated. "Your crofters, Sir Andrew, inhabit hovels which should be given over to the pigs." Her face flushed, and she moved uneasily, yet not seeking to fly.

Sir Andrew was boiling with rage. "Do you blame me for this, madam?" he cried.

She answered, "Blame rests with some hands, which are not God's. The earth is the Lord's and the fulness thereof, and He has given largely of His riches into the hands of some men—His stewards—and woe will come to such of them as unjustly abuse the power."

"Heard we ever the like!" was all the attacked knight could for a little while utter. He had not been bearded like this, even at political meetings, which had formerly been quiet enough, under the power he had been accustomed to exercise.

"You have learned in a Radical school, madam," Sir Andrew said, "and with such politicians I hold no converse. Perhaps the schoolmaster at Morven—a poacher and a demagogue—I will lay hold of him some day —is answerable for your opinions—perhaps for your birth," he continued with a sneer, as he emptied the contents of a large glass of wine, and took some grapes to himself with a stare of unconcern.

Ellen was stung to the marrow. She only said, "The schoolmaster is responsible for neither my feelings nor my birth."

"Who is then?" growled the knight.

Mrs Jenkins rose and motioned for Ellen to follow her, but her guest was heated with rage, and cried "No, no; let us hear."

It was no moment for softness on the part of Ellen. She felt in the moment the weakness of her sex, and her friendlessness, but she resolved against their bearing her down. "When I know the ground of the right to question me about my family, which Sir Andrew assumes to himself, I will answer him."

"Miss Lee is the niece of Mr Oliver Arnot, a farmer at Morven. She has been bred in the country and forgets herself," said Mrs Jenkins, in a fever of suspense.

Sir Andrew looked again at Ellen, who stood confronting him with a paled face, and eye that seemed suppressed in its fire. He uttered not another word, motioning with a nervous move of his hand that the discussion was ended. A terror seemed to hold possession of him ; it might be shame, or the rush of mingled emotions through his brain, which paralysed for a moment his energies. He was vanquished, though it might not be by the attitude of her who had confronted him. Ellen had turned and gone her way out of the room, when the expression on the knight's face awoke to one of hard compressed hate. He, too, rose uneasily, as if his heart had ceased for the time to go on with its common unconcerned beating, or that at last a chord from some mysterious hand had informed him of the presence of such an organ. The jeweller was overflowing with anger at her who had brought this pang to so great a customer, and cursed her impudence. He saw Sir Andrew out, and the knight struggled in uneasy step along the deserted square, but not till he had hissed into the ear of Jenkins, "Turn that woman away at once ; she will destroy your trade."

Ellen was sent away at once.

CHAPTER XVI.

ALAN MACALPINE returned sadly to Morven, the justice of his attachment to Ellen confirmed in the strengthened light of her unselfish character. As the summer declined, to him the autumn wind moaned through the trees with a dull eerie sound which had little in it of its former music, the river's leaping waves looked cruel and harsh, the keen air was cold and piercing.

In Alan's hopes as a lover, he could only dream of a distant and uncertain future. " And fleeting time," said he to himself, " must be a first element in all our calculations of happiness ;" and then he repeated the lines of Andrew Marvel :—

> " Had we but world enough, and time,
> This coyness, lady, were no crime ;

But at my back I always hear
Time's winged chariot hurrying near ;
And yonder all before us lie
Deserts of vast eternity."

He thought of all that might occupy Ellen's mind. If his mistress, like some heroine in the romantic tales he had read of, insisted upon his coming to woo her with a glory bright as the colours of the rainbow, their union could never be, for he was settled in simplicity.

Activity, which is the great panacea against man's restless spirit, dispelled occasionally Alan's sombre musings. He had set straight the crooked causes of the strange onslaught into the church. He had disseminated the meeting's rebuke of Sir Andrew's tyrannic threat. He had laboured in the matter of the establishment of the new school. He had formed an association of agriculturists, consequent upon the meeting held in the church ; and he had already read a paper upon the breeding and diseases of cattle and sheep, and drawn out the farmers and shepherds to discuss, in their own way, their own experience as against his theories. But he was not employed in converting Lucretia Mar to Radicalism.

During the summer Alan had seen the heiress of Morven only at a distance. It was none of his seeking that she was interested in his society ; yet it was strange that their last interview should be followed up by an absence, on her part, of even friendliness. It was well, perhaps, Alan still felt the approaches of the heiress of his family estates as fraught with danger to him.

Notwithstanding, Alan had cause to be offended at her conduct, which intimated an utter disregard of his own feelings. His position was this :—She had made overtures of an unmistakable character,—not woman's privilege, according to rule, in any case,—but made, and not resented, because of Alan's sympathy with every reasonable advance of the sex towards equality with man; and she had thereupon, and without a word, cast off the very sight of him! While he had not repelled, he had given signs of his negation. Yet he knew at their parting that she treated this as nought; and he believed her to be playing a heartless game to relieve that ennui for which a new set of politics was at one time to be a cure.

> "In glowing health, with boundless wealth,
>   But sickening of a vague disease,
> You know so ill to deal with time,
>   You needs must play such pranks as these."

Lucretia Mar had been occupied with Ballatruim, Ogilvie, and Hamilton. They had discovered her interest in the political movements of the county; and under pretence of discussing these, their attendance upon her was assiduous. It amused her to read the spirit of the hunters of the heiress through the civilities of the gentlemen of the world. How easily she saw to the bottom of the characters of Ballatruim and Hamilton! How pliant was

Ballatruim, how bending was Hamilton, when she chose to lead the way! In the rollick of Ogilvie alone did she see something real— which it appeared to her might there exist because there was no pretence of it.

"Might I ask," inquired Ballatruim of Miss Mar, as they had sat alone for a little time one day, in the autumn, in her room at Morven Castle, "how the daughter of so staunch a Tory comes to hold principles so Liberal?"

Miss Mar was arrested in her careless glance at an illustrated book of travels she held in her hand. She looked straight at Ballatruim, and did not leave off for the space of a minute. The Laird winced considerably.

"Well, I may now consider myself half a Scotchwoman," she answered; "and I adopt her privilege of answering a question by asking another :—How comes it that Ballatruim has become so mild in his Toryism and in his abuse of Whiggery?"

"You are the cause, Miss Mar."

" What!—I the cause? I—denounced by
Mr Ogilvie as a person of no principles !"

" But not by me."

" You are then truly to take the field in the
Whig interest ?"

" If I have your sanction."

" Sir ! "

" It is you, Miss Mar, who have led me to
think thus, to rehabilitate the old principles in
the dress of the new era, to cast away the old
and worn-out dogmas, to march with the progress of the human intellect, to surrender to
the inevitable : and I became a Liberal, pressed
into the conviction by the force of your example and precept."

" I disavow the imputation of proselytizing,"
she repeated, coolly.

" And I have the best hopes of my success."

" What success ? " she inquired.

" That which writes M.P. with it," he said,
excitedly serious.

Lucretia Mar had the vulgar element in her

own composition, yet she now felt that the man Ballatruim was a vulgar creature. It was evident to her that Ballatruim was attempting to dazzle her with his magic letters.

"Have you sufficient support to ensure this?" she inquired, as coolly as before.

"Yes; that is, if I have Colonel Mar's interest with me."

"And how to secure that?"

"By my acquiring what I regard as a greater prize than any honour."

"And that is"——

"Yourself."

"You have acquired me already, so far as I can serve you,—which is not at all."

"Good heavens! Miss Mar, why will you misrepresent to yourself my plain-spoken hopes. Until I met you I never knew woman whom I—upon my life—thought worthy to seek; I am not worthy of your hand; I feel it: but if time, energy, labour, devotion, can do anything towards rendering myself capable of

fulfilling the duties of a true husband to such
as you, I can vouch for my attainment in the
end.   Do not remember against me that horrible scene in the church : I was mad—I was
not myself.   Oh, Miss Mar—Lucretia—it is to
you I look for happiness; without you the
world is a blank.   I can offer you the union
of an old family, with a good inheritance ;
before you, I trust, is even increased rank—
why not the sway of the wife of a statesman ?
Will you not then be moved ?   Say, for the
sake of heaven, that I may hope."

The speech may have been rehearsed. The
listener thought so.

"Your fluency is against you, Ballatruim ;
it is fatal to the highest designs of oratory
and art. You have been too much accustomed
recently to the district meetings."

Ballatruim turned aside to hide his savage
spleen, the presence of which it was not otherwise in his power to conceal.

"I cannot believe, Miss Mar, in the rivalry

of a man who would bring you down to his own mean level," he said, between his teeth.

"Nor do I," she answered, cold as ice.

"You have not even answered the question I first put to you ; and yet I have replied to yours, with but a sorry rejoinder," cried the laird, scarce knowing what to say.

"Repeat the question, if you insist upon your right." She felt her own superiority.

"Who brought you to Liberalism ?"

"Mr Alan Macalpine."

Ballatruim got an answer he did not expect would be given. Recently, while Miss Mar had only been amusing herself, he had fondly fancied she might even be his convert. He could only turn again and conceal his spleen. But he could bear a thousand insults upon such an errand as this, calling them flashes of his mistress's humour. He had failed, but he would return. She who was so great an heiress, and the possession of whom he deemed the means of securing his highest aggrandisement, could not be abandoned on account of a frown! But he hated Alan Macalpine with all the devilish pettiness of his small heart.

No one had been more industrious to endeavour to dissipate the ill feeling of the landed magnates towards Colonel Mar than Sir Andrew Cameron. It had grown to be the chief object of his daily hopes to see his nephew and heir, Captain Hamilton, united to the heiress of Morven. How pleasing it was to his imagination, the thought of his handling the bulky rent-roll of Morven. Colonel Mar could not live long; the captain disliked business; and it would fall to the knight to have in his hands a vast increase of territorial possession.

When Sir Andrew made his frequent appearances at Morven, in the real character of wooer for his stiff nephew, Miss Mar advanced in all the riches of her person, as she had met Ballatruim with a mental attire addressed to his priggishness.

" I am surprised to find you an advocate for matrimony, Sir Andrew, who have thriven so well on single blessedness." She said this in answer to Sir Andrew's news, that the eldest son of Glenballoch's neighbour-laird had married the daughter of the Edinburgh brewer; and he approved of every young person marrying as soon as they could feather their nest, and of the union of blood and wealth.

" I wonder," thought Lucretia to herself " which of us is the blood," as the consciousness of the old man's drift could scarcely be concealed from her.

" I do approve of it notwithstanding," Sir Andrew replied, rising hastily with some anxiety; "and I will see Colonel Mar now regarding a proposal I have to make to him, which concerns us all. In my own case I will never marry; no; sooner would I—— Well, well—never mind; my case is not yours, nor Frank's there"—and the voluble knight disappeared, while he pointed with his fingers first to Miss Mar, then to his nephew, indicating that they were left together to promote tender relations.

Captain Francis Hamilton was a cold man—an obstinate and vain one—yet the gallant officer had stuff in him not altogether displeasing even to Miss Mar. He did not flinch from the situation to which his uncle had brought him. The wall was before him, but how to storm it and plant the standard upon the conquered citadel?

Miss Mar sat at a little distance on the opposite side of the table from him, too experienced in defence to be under much trepidation at sight of the enemy in array of battle. The gallant officer was too much concerned with his mode of attack to heed the seductive aspect of the prize he coveted.

The mountain air had that day given to the cheek of the dark woman a freshness as of fair life which it usually wanted. Hers was not that beauty of complexion which can afford to

be without adornment; but nature, always com-
pensating, often gives an advantage to such
adorned complexions, and over that favoured
one which needs none, when that one tries to
compete with the aid of art. The flowers that
had been thrown in her slightly shaken hair,
which had been played with by the morning
breeze, the handkerchief which still lay loosely
on her neck after her morning ride, contributed
even a little, with the effects of the exercise in
which she had been engaged, to give a complexion, and an ease—or abandon—to her appearance which it often wanted. To-day she
ought to have appeared beautiful in the eyes
of Captain Hamilton, without the possession
of those rosy cheeks and cherry lips, which
were the gallant officer's real preference in his
prospect of the fair creation.

" You hear what my uncle says, Miss Mar ?
Ah—don't know but that he's firing off down-
stairs with the Colonel about you and me ;
now it strikes me he should not interfere, but

it 's like him ; it 's like the man of trade to
have his hand in all bargains,—I mean in all
things he can lay hold on.   Ah, well, to come
to the point, I 'm looking out for a wife, and
I can see nothing finer than 's here ; and, by
the immortal Mars, as we say in the army, I
have no desire to see any better woman than
Miss Mar."   The gallant officer had many
pauses ; and, receiving no answer, he went on
and floundered.

" Might I ask ? " inquired Lucretia Mar,
" what particular virtue in me it is that has
excited the esteem of Captain Hamilton ? "

" Why, all the virtues," cried Hamilton,
recovering from a sense of previous failure.

" Nay, this is flattery.   I have been learning
in a new school, Captain, to regard things as
they are, not as deception would have us believe them to be."

" By gad, Miss Mar, we are not going to
quarrel over the point whether you be more
modest than charitable—more witty than wise."

"I am beaten at this point, and retire on the main, Captain," she said, gaily, taken by surprise at the wit of the other.

"And there to surrender, I hope."

The only literature the Captain possessed was a volume of old comedies of the Restoration. His knowledge of love-making had been got there; he could imitate the heroes of Wycherley after a fashion.

"Captain Hamilton must first show me what strength he brings to the attack," she said.

"By gad, Miss Mar, you see it all before you," the Captain ejaculated. "I am all for love."

"So in my case," she replied. "I am altogether dependent upon Colonel Mar; and at any moment, so whimsical is he, I may be reduced to a penniless position. That I understand to be your position, Captain. With one of the parties independent, it may be well; but with both dependent, as we are, the thing were madness to enter upon marriage."

The Captain's face fell. "Gad, there is some

truth in this," he said, quickly. "But you are the Colonel's only child," he continued, with animation.

"As to that I can say nothing," answered the lady, mysteriously, while her head drooped as if she feared it might be otherwise.

"Gad!" cried the Captain; "you do not mean to say that Colonel Mar was ever married to any other woman than your mother, and had a family by her. How horrible!"

"Eh, Captain! how can that be? there is nothing wrong in having been twice married?" she said, coolly, enjoying the sham of her suitor, aroused to his best pitch.

"But there is, though. I call it shocking, repulsive to the best feelings of the heart, and subversive of the tenderest memories. You are the eldest daughter, Miss Mar?"

"I did not say that I had occasion to experience any thought concerning a father's second marriage," she replied.

"Ah! then you are an only child ?—so far as you know ?"

"Just so ; so far as I know. You see I desire to conceal nothing which may affect our relative decisions. I am flattered by a proposal of marriage coming from a gentleman for whom I entertain a regard, and I give it the consideration it deserves by treating of our circumstances frankly. You have candidly stated yours, and I also prefer to exhibit the barrenness of the land you come to. I am bound to tell you, though for your own keeping as a gentleman, that I fear sometimes Colonel Mar will not settle the estate upon me. I have been bred with means unlimited," she continued ; "and what you observe in my Highland residence gives you no idea of my necessities ; and until I am forced to abdicate, I intend to live as I have done. It is not the case," she continued, in a manner which became extremely haughty, "that men deny themselves the gratification of any of their

luxurious tastes for the sake of woman's love,
nor do I think she ought to be called upon
to make sacrifices for such as is theirs."

It was dawning upon the suitor that her
fears concerning her succession were assumed.
Had he possessed the spirit of a true man,
the lady had now given him the chance of
casting aside these base calculations. But
the man had not a soul above them. He
played with the cover of the album which lay
on the table, without saying a word.

"Take a look at the rhyme on the first leaf,"
Miss Mar said.

"I have read it before," he answered, after
reading the lines—a lie given in the hope of
blinding Miss Mar to his perfect understanding
of the mercantile relations of their treaty.

"It has greatly influenced Colonel Mar,"
she continued. "It is an old prophecy in
the family of Macalpine, which has been
more than once put to the test, and without fail. Roderick Macalpine has already

intimated legal proceedings to set aside Colonel Mar's purchase."

This completed the gallant officer's discomfiture. He saw in the garden below Sir Andrew and the Colonel in conversation, and took advantage of it to hastily take his leave.

Lucretia Mar stood looking the way he went. Naturally a lady should show signs of some emotion at the conclusion of a treaty for her hand; she showed none. She rarely laughed, or she would have done so now. " Unmasked? —mask he had none. So honest a fellow I have not known." Once upon a time such a man as this would have had attraction for her. She revolted now from the grovel exposed, in naked impurity, with nonchalant audacity.

Alan Macalpine meanwhile had avoided intimacy with former acquaintances, not because he was poor, but because he felt he had nothing in common with them. With a few

reasonable men (such as always respect honest
conviction, and detest all rabidness) he had required to make no change because of his
altered position. Some of these former friends
he had come in contact with in connection
with Colonel Mar's school, and they had had no
hesitation in resuming former intimate relations
with Alan, since they found he exhibited none
of the painful sense of pride, struggling with
evil fortune, such as they had expected of a
Macalpine. With these gentlemen he stood in
high estimate, while he made no concealment
of his humane politics, but referred to them
manfully when courtesy permitted. With the
mass of the social life of the county he had,
however, done, as it had done with him. It
was with the plain, simple, honest sons and
daughters of the mountain side that he found
most fellowship.

The school-house was now completed, and
Colonel Mar requested Alan to meet him and
a few of the other heritors upon the premises,

that the arrangements might be inspected finally. When Lucretia Mar heard of this intended meeting, she, with the boldness of her character, resolved to be present. " I am embarrassed," she said, " if I pass him, as I must do often ; it will give me an opportunity of breaking off." Thus it was that her chilled passion could permit her to reason with herself. She strangled the thought—" Would to heaven I were free to act as I choose."

It was both in word and deed that the coolly resolving woman was to indicate that their ways lay different. There was to be a feast at Morven Castle, and she would show Alan that their roads lay apart for ever, by purposely passing him over in the invitations.

It was a cold harsh winter afternoon, when two or three carriages, and a horse or two, stopped at the door of the new school building. Colonel Mar had arrived first, while his daughter, on horseback, made her appearance after the party had wholly assembled. They were already engaged in examining the testimonials of the different candidates for the office of schoolmistress, when she entered. The gentlemen rose from their seats, though she shook hands with none.

Her air was that of the grand dame. It was only the activity of her spirit that *seemed* to have brought her to condescend into exhibiting her interest in the humble affairs of a village school, and to sit down within its bare unhistorical walls. She glanced at the contents of the packet which was handed to her, upon which she had been asked to pronounce judgment as best qualified to determine upon the relative merits of persons of her own sex. " You are mistaken, gentlemen, in applying to me," she said. " We are fitter judges of your sex than of our own. I might be partially blinded by jealousy were I to read the contents of these papers." There was a sneer in her words. And what was one there to understand by it ?

"In judging of our sex there is the greater danger of a lady becoming totally blind by the influence of a still stronger feeling," cried a jolly laird; while the whole party laughed, and Miss Mar, astonished at wit coming from such a quarter, could scarce conceal her annoyance.

"There are no fashionable accomplishments needed in the teachers of poor children; singing, no doubt, though I had hopes you would confine the education to washing, scrubbing, and cooking, in addition to reading, writing, and arithmetic," she said, in an imperious manner.

"Your conception is an excellent one, Miss Mar, but we have not the means of completing it; the accomplishments you refer to must be learned so far as possible at home in the meantime," said Alan, annoyed by the spleen which had gathered in the heiress of Morven during her months of silence, and was now venting itself.

It was not jealousy that she came to labour

under, as it was not hate. She was too self-sustained to be jealous, and believed too much in her own power to dread the serious rivalry of an impoverished relation of Farmer Arnot. It had pleased her only to think that Ellen Lee might be sufficiently formidable in personal attraction to make her own conquest of Ellen's quondam lover a gratification to her vanity.

Even now she felt growing within her, when he had spoken, that liking for Alan which was the only likeness of love she ever knew, and she called to her aid her obstinate will to put it down. She came to scoff, and loved.

"I thought you had fixed on a governess," she said, after Alan had spoken. " I heard the situation had been offered to a niece of Mr Oliver Arnot, a young person of your own acquaintance."

"She was asked to apply," answered Alan, boldly; though his natural modesty seemed to struggle for the mastery. He exhibited his relations with the applicant to every one present.

Lucretia Mar enjoyed his confusion. It was vulgar and cruel of her, and had she wavered in the scale of Alan's appreciation of her character, this of itself could not fail to turn it against her. There is a temper which may be fierce and yet never indelicate. Rudeness is brutality.

"She did not think the situation equal to her deserts?" said Miss Mar. The sneer was within, without venturing this time to appear. She had had a triumph. She would be merciful.

"That may be assumed," answered Alan, with more appearance of calmness than he felt. "How does it happen?" he asked himself, "that I am to be alternately baited and cajoled by this woman?"

"My feeling is to leave the choice entirely to Mr Macalpine," she continued. "Having selected one who is superior to candidature, he is most likely to procure one equal to it."

An ordinary young gentleman would have

thrown up a position of charitable laborious-
ness so thankless when it gave a handle to the
gibes of the directorate. Alan did nothing,
however, but wait the decision of the others.
Colonel Mar asked him with diffidence—sitting
on burning ashes, as he afterwards told his
daughter he did, through her sneering manner
—to undertake the office of selector. Alan
agreed, and thanked Colonel Mar for the confidence throughout that the officer had shown
in his assistance.

Miss Mar rose and turned on her heel, and
the business which had drawn the meeting
being over, Colonel Mar and the others followed.

"Stay, Lucretia," cried the Colonel, as she
was about to mount on horseback, and the
gentlemen were making their way towards
their conveyances which waited in advance ;
" where is Mr Macalpine ? "

"How should I know; you best know the
cause of his absence," she answered, with a

look of mingled pride and anger, such as she seldom exhibited to her father.

"Have you not, then, invited him to Morven?"

"No," she cried.

"Do so now, then," said the Colonel, sharply.

"It is too late now. What care have either you or I for this man?" she continued. "You seek the lame and the halt for me, and when I compassionate them, you insist that they be-gone; and again you bid me restore them to favour. I cannot do so,—this cripple I cannot receive."

She sat boldly in the saddle, while the hypochondriac, startled by the sound of the heavy boot of Alan upon the stair behind him, dragged along to his carriage. She had never dared to controvert his will as she did now; but she was not altogether wrong, he confessed to himself. He felt there was some real iniquity in what he had done concerning her and Macalpine. The guilty indecision which he felt had crept upon him in his retired home struck him with full force, and he resolved to do penance. "She does not know me, this daughter," he said to himself. He feared, too, that Alan had overheard some of his daughter's speech, which was loudly spoken.

The last five words of her speech had indeed been distinctly overheard by Alan, who had also partly overheard what had gone before, as he stood locking the side door. " This cripple I cannot receive." These words were used respecting himself. The continued halt of Colonel Mar and his daughter, and the half turned body of the former, as if at first unde-cided as to returning to Alan or joining his party, showed Alan what father and daughter were discussing.

As the son of Macalpine descended through the shaggy wood which divided the place he had just left from his home, there arose in his breast a deeper pain by the insolent pride of the daughter of his father's successor which had

wounded him. He could not place her beneath
his resentment and his interest. He had found
himself striving to know her. But to-day he
went as one whose heart rages at the collision of
an element antagonistic to its calm, placid, and
self-approving hopes. His proud spirit seemed
rising as with a wilder, stronger energy after
a slumber, ready, too, to find pleasure in the
storm, and to take the sting out of the defier.
He saw the effigy of himself in this hour of
pain as he entered his desolate house, riding
with a fleet, mad-like enjoyment, over the
obstacles in his dark, frowning course.

CHAPTER XVII.

THE constraint between the Macalpines, father and son, which arose much from the thoroughly impracticable and selfish character of Roderick, was not always maintained, as we have seen. The father seeing the son in a mood which seemed writhing under any sense of defeat, would take the opportunity of trying to steal a march on him through his sensitiveness to the dangers of the career which he had set before him,—a career the father disdained. Alan, though he could be no victim to the pangs of disappointed ambition as its common votaries are, was ambitious after his own particular fashion; he was eager for the success of the way of life that he was working out for himself; should it fall through and he be left in the cold bed of isolation, he would surely suffer. A restless and active mind will not allow its possessor to repose in mere dream-land, however richly it be imbued with the poetic faculty ; and it was in truth no smooth thing always for Alan Macalpine to lead the plain-looking life which had become his choice. He might almost have felt the pride of the pioneer; but he was solitary in the Morven hills ; there was no one with him.

Alan had recently not been fortunate with his trade in cattle, and had lost, for his slender means, a considerable sum by an adverse decision in a lawsuit with a dealer who had defrauded him. These were reverses which he bore bravely, scarcely with a murmur ; experiences, however, practically reminding him that virtue, honour, charity, and love will not of themselves preserve a man from defeat and contumely ; for he found these reverses had not only brought him loss of money, but of reputation, so superficial are the judgments of the common people of the world.

On the morning of the day following the events last related in the previous chapter, Roderick Macalpine, as he sat with his son at the homely fare provided for their breakfast, observed that the latter did not wear at all a cheerful expression, which was habitual to him in his hours of ease. The father had become more inquisitive respecting his son, as his own concerns occupied him less.

" I hear," said Roderick, " that Sir Andrew's crofters must go at Candlemas."

" It has been a threat only," said Alan, who listened to his father's statement with some apprehension.

" Tam Cameron showed me his service copy summons of removing; and at the same time quietly damned you for interfering with the laird."

" I have not interfered beyond denouncing his tyranny."

" His tyranny should have been nothing to you; you have sufficient scoundrels upon your own premises. Things are bearing hard upon us ; our wretched pittance is going, and we shall be cast in beggary unless you leave off this cursed philanthropy. You let the abomination of your own natural enemies fall upon upon you like pellets on the hide of a rhinoceros. There are these cursed Mars ; I have not disturbed them that you might marry the daughter, and now she'll have none of you, since you frequent ale-houses with stablemen, and prefer a courtship with a woman of neither birth nor fortune but "——

"Stop!" cried Alan, his indignant passion aroused ere he was aware ; for he usually treated his father's heats with discreet coolness ; "you speak of one whom you do not know."

"You despise the pride of birth, and prefer to walk in the by-roads. It is because they will not,—because they cannot muster sufficient courage, that men pretend to hug their obscurity and refuse to attain to elevation in society. You are kicking aside the ball which is at your feet; why, Alan, why? Had you not thought of retaliation upon the hypocritical villany that has trod upon us in our fall. What is love beside the victory of a lifetime? a poor, puny thing compared to the grand passion for restoration of a home of centuries."

Roderick was more really earnest, and, to the then state of his son's feelings, closer in argument than he had on previous occasions been when the subject of his style of life was brought up.

He told his father that, there being no inheritance for him, he was free from the supposed obligations attached to the receipt of it; which was a quiet hint that it was greatly the father's own wrong that was the cause why there was any necessity for him to speak as he did.

"Ah," cried the father, "would to heaven I had my life to live over again; you would not have cause to rate me so soundly!" Roderick

Macalpine generally admitted his errors—nay, his sins,—often a truer sign of hopelessness of reformation than a superficial observer of human character will credit. He looked as if Alan ought to make an admission because he had done so.

"You expect me to confess to my sins : if I am wrecked upon my own voyage, I will confess—not till then," Alan said.

"Too late! too late!" cried the father, "to seek the promised land when you are dying in the desert."

"Come," said Alan, rising from his seat, "take your gun and resume your sports; you are too much in the house lately, and have become dreary."

"Too late! I say," he repeated, while a wild fire stood in the dark eyes of the world-struck Highlander; and he rose impulsively and confronted Alan, with the boldness a prostrate man can put on in the hopelessness of his agony. "We are beggars. The means you expected from your mother's stock will not be forthcoming ; I sold the stock six months ago."

" And where went the proceeds?" inquired the son.

" Speculated with and lost ; and more—I am yet owing a debt."

Alan said nothing. He might justly have cursed the sins of his father. But why rave to the winds? He simply went forth to the open day. What had gone was the remains of the scant fortune which had come with his mother, and had been set apart through her care, though in her husband's name, for her son's benefit.

Months had passed since Alan had been within the walls of Finzean. He had only been once after having seen Ellen Lee at Tarbet. Somehow to-day he bent his steps thither ; and as he walked, the pains which would gnaw at his mind insensibly sought relief in outer objects. His mind needed diversion from its gloom ; and he found a

magic in the merry laugh and the pleasantries
of speech of the rosy daughters of the mountain side, as he went along. But he could
not have wooed one of these. It was his
own ambition, seeing them deficient in moral
elevation and ideas, to aid in raising those of
healthy heart and simple wants to be the
companions of intellectual man, and to leave
in the shades, for recovery, the dulled and
costly ladies of effete society. Yet Lucretia
Mar he had not found dull.

Jess Arnot and Tam were employed at an
inspection of a couple of cows as Alan entered.
Disease had been prevalent in the district for
some time, and the watchful care of the mistress of Finzean was constantly exercised in
the endeavour to prevent the inroad of the
epidemic. Alan heard more than once the
cry, "Tam, ye deil, what are ye aboot!" as
the ungainly youth struck too roughly the
hides of the animals.

Both mother and son were better disposed

to the laird's son since they knew that his connection with Ellen had terminated. They turned as he passed the yard, and greeted him loudly after their particular fashion.

"Tam, man, get ye a lesson frae Maister Alan; he kens mair aboot beasts than laws"— a jocular allusion to his defeat with the law-plea. "The Maister'll be gled to see you, sir; he often speirs if ye hae been up when he's been awa'; but ye're an unco stranger here noo, I tell him. Tam, tell your father Maister Alan's gaen into the parlour; he's maybe awa' i' the garden looking after the bit flowers that he maks sic a wark wi'. Gudeman, I say to him, it looks as if you thocht mair o' a nettle than a yearlin'."

Alan said that her husband knew the value of her skill over his own with the cattle.

"Ou ay; nae doot we're married for something. The man that wants maun look out for the woman that has. The wise man gets the rich fule for his wife, and the bonnie

woman gets the rich man. Baith the same 'll
no agree, Maister Alan; they 'll be knocking
their heads thegither. Ilka ane to his ain
trade, and man and wife at the same maks
fechtin'. I ken aboot doctorin' better than
Oliver Arnot. Tam, didna ye hear me?—
tell your faither. Quick! ye muckle lumberin'
deil. Tam 'll need a bonnie wife; for though
I 'm the mither that bore him, I canna say
he's weel faur'd; but he's a shrewd chap, Tam,
and 'll no let the world aboon him; and if I
could only get a sweet, simple, kindly, workin'
lassie for him, a mither's heart would be at
peace. I had thòchts o' Ellen to him, Maister
Alan, but the lassie had her head turned a
wee, and she's noo gaen scamperin' to foreign
parts, that I ken na what's to become o' her."

Alan inquired what this meant with more
concern than the dame relished.

" Let the maister speak to you himsel'; it's
no my department to be interfering with his
fouk; for deil tak me if I say a word there.

I micht murder his black cattle, and set his
stack-yard alow, and he'd no say a syllable;
but advise him aboot his fouk, and he's the
deil himsel', gude worthy man! Gude keep's
a'!" cried the virago, as she approached the
parlour-window, " there he is, cheek-by-jowl
wi' the Colonel and Sir Andrew; there's some
deevilry aboot. Get ye in, Maister Alan, if
ye be a freind o' the maister's or mine, for he
looks reed and flustered like; and Andrew
Cameron 'll take the weak side o' him, as sure
as my name's Jess Arnot. Ye've got a gift
o' the gab; though 'gin ye pay ithers for't, ye
dinna come off sae weel. Get ye in by."

The Colonel and Oliver Arnot recognised
Alan as he approached the window; the other
scowled and looked hard at him. Alan did
not, however, stir until Colonel Mar, joined by
Arnot, beckoned him, and he then entered the
house.

Sir Andrew had the talk to himself. He
was entreating the farmer in high language.

"Arnot," he said, "you are now nothing else than a vile Whig; if you value your country, don't desert the party of the State; the rest is anarchy."

"You're mistaken, Sir Andrew," answered the farmer, "I'm a truer Tory than you are, that uphold the auld customs. Ever since I've been a man I hae held this Yule, and I'll no gie't up for ony cause, savin' ill-health or poverty. Thank God, I'm braw enough baith ways."

"What says Macalpine?" cried the Colonel, seizing his hand, which Alan would have withheld. He whispered into Alan's ear—"Forget, man, a mistake; we shall make right amends yet." Evidently, from the warmth of his grasp and look, he had lodged Alan again in the centre of his chief designs.

"Sir Andrew calls upon me to have nae Yule feast this Christmas, for he fears some of the crofters' ill tempers, when met together, will breed a riot," said the farmer, addressing Alan.

" They have rarely anything to fear who act impartially," observed Alan, who now had to confront the man whose tyranny he had denounced otherwise.

" Will you answer, young sir, for any damage to my property and person when infuriated blockheads are mad with drink ?" asked the knight, with angry lower.

" But how infuriated, Sir Andrew ?—by whom ?—through what ? You may remove the cause of quarrel. Say that you refer your differences to Mr Arnot and myself, with Colonel Mar as oversman, and you will have no cause to fear riots."

" What the devil, sir ! do you presume to dictate to me in the management of my own affairs ?" shrieked Sir Andrew.

" My opinion was asked, and it has been given," answered Alan, drily, as he turned away towards the fireplace.

" I want none of it, sir," continued the other ; "and now, Arnot, you cannot refuse

me this favour—I ask it as a great favour—
one I will not forget; and hark you, between
ourselves: You have a niece, a governess, to
whom I would, for auld lang syne—cause as I
have against it—do a good turn. Grant you
me but this, and I'll get her a splendid place
abroad, with a bit of money of my own providing."

"I can provide for my ain kith and kin
mysel', Sir Andrew," answered Oliver Arnot,
disgusted with the commercial spirit of the
knight, while his face flushed the more, as if
there had been cruelty in the speech made to
him concealed from common ears.

" I will make it five hundred pounds," whispered the knight, heedless of the other's apparent indignation.

"I do not wish that my niece should leave
me," said the farmer, aroused by the eagerness
with which Sir Andrew pressed the not incon-
siderable bribe.

" You will do this, Arnot; make your own

terms. I know, my old friend, you are now well off; but it's ill parting with the gear before it's done its full turn; I know you lost money by the bank failure."

"I'll neither gie up my Yule nor my niece to your providing, Sir Andrew—hear ye that? Your offers, man, are naething else than insults, tho' ye havena the delicacy to see it." This last sentence was spoken loudly as the farmer rose from his seat, his jolly countenance vexed and heated more.

"Colonel Mar," cried the knight, "have you nothing to say to this?"

"I doubt if more can be said on the matter than that the giver of the feast must see that his guests behave themselves," answered the Colonel.

"Is it possible!" exclaimed the knight; "it is but half an hour since you expressed yourself strongly against the danger and injustice of your tenant interfering with my people in this manner."

" I see the affair in a new light," said
Colonel Mar. " I fear you over-estimate the
danger."

" My respecs, gentlemen," cried Mrs Arnot,
who now entered the room. " I heard ye
speakin' high, a' aboot the bit Yule. Lord, Sir
Andrew, the proof o' the puddin' 's the preein'
o't! So 'gin ye dreed treason in our barley
bree ye maun just come and mak fou aff 't.
What's a' the steer aboot; a wheen carls at a
lilt! Lord be here, it 's no the bluid that 's
bred on some land that sets them on to the
deil! Do ye say riotin', Sir Andrew, amang
your fouk? True, there 's bonnie men been
among them, but they 've grown aff ither corn,
for it 's but sma' meal whaur the breath 's oot
o' the land. Takin' the last bodle oot o' the
rig betters naither man nor beast; and the
sheep winna live on sticks or heather, nae mair
nor milk will be got oot o' twa cows fed on a
wheen tufts ca'd grass. Gude preserve 's a'
frae coming to be puir bodies, that pay mair

rent than there's meal or sheep for, an' the
puirer the waur likin' to move! For I'm
thinkin' 'gin they waur but half better aff than
they are, they'd pou doun the bit rickets, and
aff to the far wast. O Lord! Sir Andrew,
yer bairns'll ne'er be ta'en up for maleecious
mischief: ye've tether't ower weel an' keepit
them on gruel ower lang, that they should
brak yer banes wi' chappin' sticks!"

There is no saying how long the lady might
have continued in this strain, to the amusement of Alan, and partially so to Oliver Arnot
and Colonel Mar, but to the horror of Sir
Andrew. There was a wild obstreperous pith
in the manner as well as matter of Mistress
Jess which it was impossible to silence by
ordinary means.

Sir Andrew knew, however, something of
her of old, and was sufficiently aware of her
hard character to know that the lady had her
price. He had risen and approached her as
she addressed him near to the door. "Come,

mistress, you and I are auld acquaintances :
speak me a little fairer, and we'll not cast
out." Here he approached her ear, and spoke
to it alone—" What if we should turn the Yule
into a marriage feast ?"

" Eh, Sir Andrew, that would be a bonnie
fray !" cried the dame, loudly.

" You have a fine chap of a son, and your
goodman has got a bonnie niece ; let's marry
them that day, and I'll taste your barley
bree, and put down five of the hundred pound
notes when the parson has tied the couple.
Tam would make his fortune with a little
capital in the far west, mistress ; he is just the
man, with such a wife, for a property I'll get
him in Illinois."

" Ay, ay, Sir Andrew," answered the wily
Jess, " may be ye wad mak it ten o' thae notes."

" Now, don't be too greedy," said the knight,
suspiciously, trembling at the fear that there
might be strange motives imputed to his seeming generosity.

" Ye say weel, Sir Andrew, when your pouch gapes, for it's like to tak lock-jaw gin the mow be stressed!" cried the woman. She bore an old grudge to the knight; and for once, love of gold and of success to a favoured scheme were in the background to her enjoyment of a moment's full retaliation.

Sir Andrew had gone by the time her speech was ended. He was utterly put to rout.

" I had hopes," said Alan to the farmer, when the others had gone, " that these old people, who have worn their frames on the hard soil of the glen, might have partaken my hospitality. It is but too true that they are to be thrust out; but I am too poor—poorer than I thought I was yesterday—and I must forego the pleasure and the mark of goodwill."

" Hold!" cried the farmer, " ye've had your will, which they maun take for the deed. But this I'll do for ye, as sure as my name is Oliver: every soul of a man among them come up to years 'll feed i' my big barn on Yule nicht, and sing 'Auld lang syne.'"

"I fear," said Alan, "it will be the farewell of 'Cha till mi tuilich.'"*

"Be what it will, they are welcome; and if gude beef and barley bree will make them heed their sorrow less, the thing will be done."

"I hear of another emigrant," said Alan, unmistakably showing, by the sadness of his tone, to whom he referred.

"Ellen," said Arnot, as he turned away his face.

"But why is this?—why does she go?" inquired Alan. It was plain that Arnot was disturbed, that a heavy trial was put upon the generously disposed man. He addressed Alan by his Christian name, which he had not done since the laird's son was a boy leaving for college. There was affection in his tone, though he felt that Alan had come between

* "I return no more."

him and his own projected happiness, in the marriage of Alan and his niece. They turned into the garden, where the farmer was accustomed to linger many leisure moments, in remembrance of incidents there in a previous summer, when he felt happier than now. Being winter, it was dark and bare, though relieved by evergreens and a conservatory of rare and favourite plants.

"There," said Arnot, pointing to arrays of once flourishing flowers as they entered, "this was her work, but it was soon over. How I loved that lassie!"

"Can it be true that she flies altogether from you—from me? I have believed in our marriage for all that has been." Alan looked eagerly at Arnot.

"She goes to India, I'm thinking, in a month," answered Arnot, with as much unconcern as he could assume.

"She does wrong," said Alan, firmly. "False notions of her duty have enslaved her. Why are we all to be made unhappy when there is no reason for it, except a barrier set up by the insane pride of others?"

"Na, na! ye have no spoken Ellen's heart there: it's a right sense o' duty—real love— that's the cause o' all. I canna vanquish ye wi' words, but my ain heart tells me the lassie does nobly, not to cripple the son of Macalpine. Na, na!—say nae mair. I ken ye would be true to her—mair than true to what ye pledge for; but ye'd be wrang. The lassie has my ain mind wi' her."

"But why, Arnot, not keep her with you? If I am the cause, I so prize her happiness that I rather will abandon the wish of my heart. Say that I drive Ellen Lee from her home, and she will never see me there."

"It canna be," cried the farmer. "She thinks it a' wrang what she did, and keeps off the sight of it. It's God's truth ye yerself aye call for that ye force me to tell."

"Then she would leave her own land—her

nearest, best, perhaps only friend—that she might forget me! And I must be her murderer! Henceforth we are as strangers. I will not seek her; and if I meet her, she will have nothing to fear."

Arnot reflected. His soft heart was hurt with the pain he witnessed.

"Alan, you and I hae been auld friends, and will, I hope, for a' that's been, be to the end o' the chapter; ay, my days are getting to the sma' end. Scarcely an hour's happiness have I kent syne Ellen left me. There would, nae doubt, be cheer for me did she come. Ye may yet be Ellen's freend in thae years to come, when Oliver Arnot totters aboot, or is laid i' the earth, and ye sit i' the auld hall, laird o' Morven."

"She may come," said Alan, encouragingly, feeling more keenly how much his friend's happiness depended on the situation of Ellen at his own side.

"God grant it; but I fear no."

" I can do no more," said Alan, sadly. " I have done too much ; justice may be avenged upon me."

" Ye have cast your bread upon the waters, and it will return to ye, though it be in other guise," suggested Arnot, while he looked with a pained but kindly emotion upon the calm, pale face of Alan. 'Though the struggle was over, he knew that in Alan's deeply reflective life the pain and sorrow, as the joys, were not of the moment, but were of his being—one with it, never gone.

Had Alan been the mere man of the world, his self-reliance and resources would not have this day permitted him to sorrow as he did, cut off, as it seemed, finally and for ever from the sweetest hope of his days. With all the strength of his reason, the sensibility and romance in his nature once aroused were extreme. Ellen never attained the heights he did. Her loving nature was inclined to the domestic. The Celt in Macalpine permitted no smothering of the heroic hopes, which would break out—noiselessly it might be—but occasionally glowing with refined fire. And here was the object of his tenderest hope cast from him for ever!

CHAPTER XVIII.

THE great event of the "dead o' the year" in the quiet Morven district for years, had been the Yule feast of Oliver Arnot. The whole inhabitants of the parish participated in the anticipations and realizations of the day, whether they partook of the particular bounties of Mr Arnot or not. There were meetings and little festive gatherings in the village, but all thought of what went on at Finzean. The father of Oliver Arnot had been a severe ascetic, who was for shaving down the gayer emotions to the lowest minimum compatible with existence. His mother was the opposite in character, and possessed all the fine feelings which her son and daughter had inherited. It was the reaction against the dull teaching of his father, and the equally dull condition

F

of the proprietory in the neighbourhood, after
Laird Macalpine's fall, that set the childless and
wealthy Oliver Arnot to make merry once a
year with as much of his neighbourhood as
he could entertain. To partake of it was to
many to be distinguished.

The small bent bodies of the humbler agriculturists, who—in blue coats with long swallow
tails and brass buttons, and knee breeches—sat
tapping their snuff "mulls," discussing, with
a meek slow-paced gravity, the weather, the
season, and the produce of their stern soils,—
felt on the occasion a gratification to which
they were generally strangers. From all the
"airths" came the farmers of the Morven
estate, and their wives, sons, and daughters.
These comprised the chief guests, with acquaintances from other properties in the
parish, or living in Morven village, and a few
crofters on Sir Andrew Cameron's property,
who were in the parish, and had been accustomed to work on the Finzean farm. These

last, and the landlord's own servants, sat at the lower ends of the tables. The buggy, the drosky, the gig, or the common cart had been in use all the afternoon to convey, if not the farmer himself, his smiling rosy-cheeked wife and daughter, who, arrayed in finery partially concealed by shawls and wrappers, lolled in their seats with a great deal of simple vanity, copying the gentility of which they had had glimpses now and then at church, or on visits from the ladies of the proprietory. No such charge of being a copyist could be made against the sturdy farmer himself—neither in dress nor in manners did he strut in remembrance of the style of the laird ; if he got on any occasion drunk as a lord, it was not because the lord got drunk, but because he himself relished the means which led to that undesirable end.

This year the party at Finzean was to be made larger than usual, by the addition to the numbers of Sir Andrew's crofters, somewhat

to the annoyance of the farmers, who measured
their own consequence at a very high standard
as compared with the broken-spirited owners
of a cow, a couple of· sheep, and a tumble-
down hovel.   They were, however, mollified
when they learned that this portion of the
party would be confined to the barn ; and they
merely laughed at the good-humoured simplicity of their fellow-tenant and friend, the
maker of the feast, in being induced by the
" enthusiast," Alan Macalpine, to invite such
" puir creturs."   " Had he sent them the beef
and the cheese to their ain places," said they ;
" but that *they* should dance and fiddle ! maist
o' the bodies hadna manners, let alane the
legs, to take the floor at a penny wedding."

Alan's most pleasurable thought for some
days before had been, that those old residenters
of the glens, now to part from them for ever,
were to form part of the guests at the Yule.

It was too true that the fickle people held
just now a grudge against Alan, and he knew

it was in vain to seek to remove it at present.
Although they knew on the day they came to
Finzean that Alan was at the bottom of the
kindness, there was no alteration in their worn
minds removing the spite they bore him.

The day of the feast was as fine as winter
day could be ; the hoar frost had covered the
herbage with its silver crystals, and the ice
stood thick upon the silent pools of the river ;
the sun was strong in the clear azure air, and
all was bright and glad. It was a day when
youth runs in the veins of the growing old,
and the frowning night is forgotten.

In the large room of the house sat down
the jolly farmers with their wives and families.
Filled with health and good humour, the table
was soon in a roar. The noise was indeed
great, not hubbub ; but the bodies of such
well-fed people evolve the motions of their
minds with a demonstrative force which is
the reverse of refined. Happy, happy they,
rolling backwards and forwards, with loud

laughing chorus at their own pleasure and the reflection of it in their neighbour's face ; telling the tale for a hundredth time of a market adventure, or of a rich gain on stock, or viewing the round form of a rustic belle they were to seize in the dance.

But look ye to the weary labourer who lingers in passing the quick-come revels. There in the outhouse sat they, men who had been long in the strath and beside the hills, who were to be driven forth. In their half-broken backs, dull blear eyes, and wasted faces and forms, were living only struggle, penury, and care.

The soul is in danger by satiety or by want. There is hope for moderation; from its ranks, where equality and freedom dwell, springs more regularly the flower of human valour and intellect; when its members are chastened by joining in fellowship with the great minds of the ages, then the strong limb and the iron nerve, and the active, buoyant, and simple heart, permit response to the highest demands.

After the ladies had left, Alan had occasion to speak strongly to the farmers his views about the crofters.

"If we are to preserve the nation entire, it is not by action which drives the small farmers from their native glens and hills, as it is not by that action which retains creatures in misery ground down by exactions. These splendid nurseries of ours for men and women should not be given over to the beast of the field or the bird of the air; these regions teem with the elements of happiness, and must be rendered as accessible as possible for human labour and growth, instead of being locked in utter silence. It is demanded in the name of patriotism, of justice, in the name even of selfish economy," concluded Alan, who of course won instant and enthusiastic applause, as a sincere man always does from hearty people.

On the right hand of Oliver Arnot, according to wont, Alan was seated. He had come in a mood such as he was in when he left the party at the school-house. He was not the long enduring dreamer when quit of the practical work of the day; there was fiery energy and abandon in his blood. Always he had thrown himself in with the humours of the farmers, with whom he remained a favourite through all their occasional askant looks. To-day he seemed to rule the party. Never had his company been appreciated as it was now.

He had wished to join the humble party of crofters in the barn, but was prevented by the entreaties of his host. It smote Alan to the heart that while he was called on to the thick of the warm feast, there were men in the comparatively cheerless outhouse. During the night, amid all the humour to which he devoted himself, a sad shade intruded upon the brightness as he thought of these others. He might have thought of his own woes; but were they not to be cast out of their native land, while he remained on its soil yet honoured compared with them, for whom no one had real compassion.

About seven o'clock dinner was over, and the guests went to an upper room, where they were supplied with bohea. The room down stairs was meantime cleared with that alacrity which servants engage in to the full when they are to partake in the forthcoming benefits. In the large hall where the party had dined, dancing, blind man's buff, and other enjoyments, would commence later. Old and young would join in making their heels clamp on the oaken floor to the music of the fiddles, and the arched roof ring with the choruses of their laughter. Till an hour in the morning, late enough to permit of the neighbouring farmers to meet, as they returned, their servants making the morning visit to the cattle, their lusty frames would work to the music, and the voices they delighted in in the enjoyment of the night. It was a wild spontaneity of innocent gaiety, possessing all sound in wind and limb, not to be witnessed in many parts of the world, and which kept these Highland and Lowland bred sons and daughters the guests of Oliver Arnot the whole round of the clock and more.

As the guests sat round the long narrow room at tea, the confused clatter of tongues and cups and saucers was broken on the instant as Oliver Arnot entered, leading to the top of the room the daughter of the new laird. It was a great surprise to the farmer's guests to find Miss Mar forming one of the company, and they regarded her presence with various emotions. The excited lovers of fun considered she would damp their entertainment, while others, especially of the female sex, were gratified at her condescension, and were already scanning with a wondering awe the splendour of her apparel and ornaments. Certainly her step, as she leant on the arm of

the stout farmer, had a lofty grace, which set
off to advantage the richness of her figure.
It was not only to cause a sensation by her
awe-inspiring presence among these farmers'
wives that she came ; though she delighted
in the opportunity of receiving the worship of
her grandeur. Alan, who would at another
time have been offended in his sense of the
beautiful in woman by a manifestation of
vanity, looked upon her entrance without a
murmur : he became an optimist in the midst
of the enjoyments of the hour.

Arnot took his seat beside Alan after a
little talk with Miss Mar, whom he left to
hear the polite language of Mrs John Mac-
pherson, a lady who prided herself upon a
gentility—credit for which had been always
accorded to her—as one of ten daughters of the
late laird of Girvan, a property which had
yielded them two hundred pounds each upon
his death without male heirs.

"She would come," said Arnot to Alan. " I

told her ye had come since ye were sixteen
years, and would come maybe till ye were
sixty, though that was a stretch o' imagination; and out at once she comes with the
speech that she would follow your example if
it were convenient for me. Nae laird's daughter but herself, in this quarter, would have
come, in this winter nicht, out o' castle, out o'
bed, for our bit Yule. We maun get Wat up
to his hieland dances; the Colonel's ower quiet
for her."

"It would be unfair to suspect her of any
other design," said Alan, scarcely knowing
what he said.

"She kent ye were to be here ere she said
she would come," answered Arnot, slily laughing, as he looked at Alan and then at the
lady. "Ye maun open the ball wi' her," continued the farmer.

Alan did not speak. He listened without
hearing; he met the searching look of Lucretia
Mar—the haughty pride of power striking the

then inflammableness of his imagination to further commotion.

There, in easy dignity, in almost unconcern, with the life around her, which had been partially quieted, sat, or rather half-reclined, the heiress of Morven.

She came, then, for him—for him whom she had wantonly insulted. For an instant, it was but the work of a moment, as their eyes met, he shuddered. He felt, at first, in presence of a cold, cruel heart, selfish to the core, delighting only in personal gratification, and whose chief pleasure was to play with the feelings of one she might think worthy the game, passing her weary hours in the excitement of her passion for admiration. Yet he did not hate ; he had been purging himself of the sin, and did not give way to it now. Nay, was it not possible for him to love ? But he was in no state of mind to examine his heart to the depths. The shudder passed, he yielded to the force of events, and felt himself ready to enjoy the

fascinations of beauty and sway, which their
possessor, and his own immediate passion,
beckoned him on to. He had loved, and had
he not just lost? And was he not, then, free
to gratify the semblance of the passion, while
he retaliated on her who had injured him?

For Alan, Lucretia Mar had come. His
vision had haunted her again for many days
past, notwithstanding her strong will. The
finer spirit of the man had for her more earthy
nature a charm which she did not seek to
analyze, though she credited herself with its
possession. She had tasted, from afar off it
may be, the sweets of a more intense existence
than she knew wealth of itself could bring
her.

She came to Finzean that she might see
bodily those features which came to her so
often in her many hours of ease, and hear that
voice which had touched her with its emotional
force.

There was a stir among the tea drinkers,

who had finished their libations, and were eager to begin the real revels of the night. For an hour or more the floor was reserved for the higher class of guests, and the others would be left for some time yet in the barn. Alan rose to his feet as the old familiar buzz of expectation greeted his ear ; mechanically it seemed he obeyed the direction of his land-lord, who led him to Miss Mar. They met as if strangers, though Allan addressed her with lively observations upon the scene before them, and led her to the hall below, with an ease and elegance which indicated the power he possessed of adapting himself to occasions. His eyes sparkled with a full brilliancy, and his tall, commanding form was conspicuous in the dance for a sprightly abandon he not commonly enjoyed. There was surprise and joy in the heart of the lady as Alan led her down the dance with which they opened. The vigorous strains of the violins, playing a national air, were relieved by the soft notes of

a harp, played by an old man, whose appearance warranted Miss Mar's imagination that
he was the minstrel of story, while she might
fancy herself the haughty beauty of the castle
who had called for the solace of his lay. She
was now in a world where admiration and
worship were offered up freely. All stood
back with bated breath and awe-struck eye,
as she swept loftily down the hall, and the
rich satin dress she wore rustled upon the
oaken floor, and the plumes on her high head
waved their splendours. Her partner was no
longer distant and solemn to her ; he was
devoted as any knight of fabulous romance,
and she drank the incense of his obedience. As
they reached the foot of the hall after their keen
encounter with each couple in the old-fashioned
country dance, the enthusiasm of Lucretia
Mar broke out. " I so love this," she said ; " it
is enjoyment. How glowing are the faces of the
musicians ; and these good people are each
more impatient than another. How romantic,

too, the decorations of the walls ! This is more of true Highland life than I have yet seen."

" I envy your own situation in the scene," replied Alan. " See what it is to join in the pleasures of your own people, to be set on the throne of their hearts as it would seem for ever, even by the grace of your presence, and your keen appreciation of their happiness."

"And you," she continued, " are changed ; you are not the unbending politician, but the chief of a hundred years back, when blood, and not principles, was the bond of life and honour, and the greatest threw themselves into the warm sentiment and common action of their race."

"Though the clan has gone from the soil, and its chief too, there are still those with whom our love may be happily united," observed Alan. Alan thought of himself, and the successors of many of his own people, whom he loved, though they supplanted Macalpines. Lucretia Mar thought of herself and him.

" I should have preferred the ancient glory," she rejoined ; "you have told me it is no longer

possible to believe in it, but I will. Though
we ally ourselves to the present and to the
future, our hearts rejoice in the memories of
the past ; its noble chivalry, its romantic adventure, its devotion to love and honour, its worship of heroism. Would that we might yet wed
even the semblance of the former grandeur."

For a moment Alan might have felt upon
his sensitive heart the cold touch of an unreal
mind ; but he pushed it and the thought of it
away. Now he was on the wings of the night.

The dance had now ended, and he led his
partner to a chair which had been provided
for her at the top of the hall. It was a large
old - fashioned piece of magnificent carved
work, set upon a carpet of crimson coloured
cloth. richly embroidered ; and Miss Mar, in
seating herself in the formal place of honour,
did it no injustice. The exteriors of majesty
were represented in her erect and unbending
form, the proud command of her expression,
and her splendour of costume. As Alan leant
lightly upon the arm of her chair, he pleased

his own imagination, susceptible to the impressions of the grand, with the picture of which she was the centre.

> " Whose bright eyes
> Rain influence, and adjudge the prize
> Of wit or arms, while both contend
> To win her grace whom all commend."

" Do you think the old minstrel might sing us a song of those ancient days ? " Miss Mar inquired of Alan. "Let it be one which completes our fancy, that we are in the past of romance, rather than in the prosaic present. Cannot two or more contend for the honours of mintrelsy. I will adjudge and provide the prize." Alan went to the old man, who had sung many a lay in former days in the hall of Morven Castle. As desired, he left the corner where he and his brother musicians had been placed, and came near to the chair upon which Miss Mar was seated. The minstrel looked under his shaggy white eyebrows with a keen inquiring glance into the face of the lady, and then, with the accompaniment of his harp, commenced the ballad of the " Captive

Chief." It was a tale or legend of the early Macalpines, which the old bard sang, or rather recited, with a clearness that gave to every one in the room the full words and meaning. Angus Macalpine, the young chief of Morven, had been captured by the head of a powerful section of the Clan Grant, and kept confined in his own castle after it was taken from him. Learning of their young chief's misfortune, his next of kin, although living at a great distance, in winter time marched to render him assistance, but they were fated to meet a bloody repulse : the frozen blood of the slain uncles of Macalpine stood upon the castle steps for more than a month. But succour was at hand from another quarter. The daughter of the jealous Grant saw and loved the fallen chief, and released him. He returned to wed her; but she having told her father—who had at an earlier period desired the match—was now forbidden to listen to the vows of the natural enemy of Grant—trebly so by the numerous recent

victims of its hate ; and the daughter refused
to meet the young Macalpine, and became deaf
to his warnings. Goaded by the sense of the fearful wrong he had suffered, the young Macalpine
rallied all his powers, and cunningly attacked
Grant while reposing in a sense of security. The
result was the capture of the old chief and his
daughter ; and young Angus, true to his love for
the lady, who he knew was blameless in the feud,
married her, and regained his own lands, and
the Grant's beside, ere the thaw melted the blood
of his own people upon the steps of Morven
Castle.

"It was generous of her and of him,
minstrel," remarked Miss Mar, as the harpist
concluded his song, which had been often
enough heard in that hall, but had now been
listened to with lively application to the fortunes of the two chief persons present.

"For baith it was weel," answered the
minstrel. "Let them that can take a lesson
read one in the Captive Chief. There's but a

day for 's a', and the nicht comes when no maid's
heart will work, or the minstrel's harp play."

"You mean that had the daughter of Grant
allowed time to pass away while the young captive lay beside her feet, she would have grown
callous to his suffering?" inquired Miss Mar.

"Ye are quick at the thocht, lady. I drink
to thy future chief with the boldness of my
class," draining a goblet presented to moisten
his throat after his long recital.

Miss Mar blushed slightly, as, in recompense
of the honour the singer had done her by
addressing his song particularly to her, she
presented him with a handsome brooch which
she had herself worn. "When that chief reigns
in Morven, I will get you to repeat this song
as the first to be heard. Take this brooch, which
will keep you in remembrance of my wish."

The old man smiled, propitiated by the
kindness and attention bestowed upon him.
The sternness of his features as he sang and
at first addressed Miss Mar relaxed, and he

rose and bowed reverentially to her, approaching her chair as he did so. She was startled at his manner; for the audience, including Alan, had left her side, and it was with some concern, which deprived her for the moment of that air of ease which had sat upon her throughout, that she listened to the whisper of of the minstrel. It might have been a warning of the legend which told the fatality to the antagonists of Macalpine, for she uttered a strange laugh as she heard his first words.

Wat McTavish now appeared conspicuous on the floor, in the dress of his clan, and went through a series of performances with agility and a graceful movement of which he was master; then three other stalwart Highlanders appeared, and engaged with Wat in several dances, to the liveliest airs of the North. Another dance of the general company was again entered upon, and this time Oliver Arnot himself asked and obtained the honour of Miss Mar joining him on the floor.

"Had I returned south before this night,"
she said to Arnot, "I should have thought
poorly of the Highland people."

"Ye should have known them long ago,"
said the farmer. "They have new warld notions
noo, and care mair for the fause pride o' the
city than the old hospitalities and gaieties o'
their native straths. Tak' yer life here, Miss
Mar. Better smell the green o' the meadow,
than be at the tail o' the mistress o' the bed-
chamber. Ods, ods, had we but thae old times
back, ye'd no leave us. The country's before
the town : the one's God's ; the other only
man's."

"Your niece has not been convinced of
this," said Miss Mar, while she observed the
farmer's countenance to lose its gaiety.

"What ken ye of her, Miss Mar?" he
inquired.

"I was not long in Morven till I heard of
her," she replied.

"From that gossip Madge, I'll warrant. Ye

could hear no ill o' her, or the lips lied that said it."

"I heard of her beauty and of the admiration it created," she answered.

"She was frank and free," said the farmer, "but I fear she has suffered : these ill tongues have much to answer for; they turn aside, Miss Mar, the open hand, and close the yearning heart."

"Why is your niece not here?" inquired Miss Mar briskly, after the dance had ended, and she drew Oliver Arnot aside. "This scene would restore her spirits; she would again embrace a country life, and perhaps remain with it for all time."

"A wilfu' woman, as a wilfu' man, maun hae her way." Arnot wished to close the subject of the conversation they had again entered upon.

"I heard she was going abroad—to emigrate to a new land, and to be accompanied by"——

" I ken of no one who goes wi' her," said the farmer.

" One of them is now in the hall; now he looks towards us with curiosity at your concerned looks. Nay, do not conceal it, sir; your niece is going to be married to Mr Alan Macalpine."

" If this is to be so, I have not heard of it," said Arnot, who was puzzled and at his wits' end. What could be the speaker's motive? what truth was there in her assertion? "Na, na," he continued, after a pause, in which it occurred to him that Miss Mar's fervour seemed very much feigned, "the story's false. Take my word for the truth, Miss Mar, Alan Macalpine is a free man. Whatever has been between him and Ellen, an' it was naething mair than a summer sang, has gone—flown away as the swallow frae a wintry sough. They're ill matched that would live only on their ain heart's heat."

CHAPTER XIX.

Taking the harp from the hand of the old minstrel, who had taught Alan in former days to make use of it, the latter responded to the call for his annual song, which was generally one of his own composition. With a voice now low and plaintive, then bold and deep as the storm whose communion the singer seemed to court, as it accorded with the phases of his own temperament, he sang the verses of which the following are a portion :—

THE FAREWELL OF THE GAEL.

On the wild wave of ocean I will dream of the past ;
By the sweep of its wind, neath the lone star of night,
I will breathe the farewell to the land I have lost ;
Then, companion of storms, let it fade from my sight.

Farewell now the loved glens where my fathers repose,
And the strains of their spirits sigh low in the gale !
Ye still live in your beauty ; oh, cheer him who goes,
That yet he may join them in the bed of that vale.

For the blue heights of Morven I seek now in vain ;
In the din of the storm I yet list to the cry
    Of the warrior clans as they step on the slain
Of the enemy come on the fastness to die.

Farewell to the castle, farewell to the cottage,
The river, the loch, and the bright bloom of the hill,
    While the echoing ocean responds to my rage,
As it keeps the proud spirit in voice to it still.

The old land of our glory, the land of our name,
The home of our hearts, as to far regions we're cast ;
    To thee, then, farewell ; when the brave find their fame,
The free wave wipes the tear, and the sigh meets the blast.

When Alan began his song, a little crowd of farm-servants from the barn had assembled at the door of the hall. Conspicuous among these were many happy faces ; but those who had to face the melancholy experience which was the burden of the song, showed that they needed the sparks of defiance which the seeming moral of the song engendered. As the singer ended, there was not a whisper among the assembly, so much had he affected them by the influence of his own tender feeling for the unfortunates beside them.

An old, dark, bent, melancholy man, his

eyes wet with tears, seized Alan by the hand, and while he shook it, pointed to the direction of his comrades in the outhouse, as if he should repeat it there. " Yes, yes," said Alan, " later in the night, after your own music is over, if you wish."

As he spoke, a tumultuous shrieking without burst upon the ears of the assembly within the hall. It was the work of a moment for the farmer and Alan to press outwards to the door, and the cause of the noise was explained. The long pent-up pains of the wretched crofters had burst out, and they shrieked forth the horrors of their situation. They had now come to know the part the lairds had played in endeavouring to stop their coming, and drunk with their sorrows and rage, and with the unaccustomed fire in their ill-filled veins, they rushed out, headed by Tam Cameron, and bellowed the vengeance they intended to heap on their laird's head into the free and·clear night. Cameron was known to possess a bold, forward originality of mind, besides a powerful frame. He brandished an immense axe, as if to cut down every obstacle to his progress. His head and neck were bare, and his short and slightly bent but massive frame, possessed a litheness which seemed to indicate a new being. The party who confronted him paused as they witnessed this Hercules in action, wielding a weapon which seemed a feather in his grasp. Alan thought he might be considered answerable for the conduct of these people, who now seemed to defy their entertainer and him, and he advanced to Cameron.

"Back! son of Macalpine!" cried the half-mad leader in rapid Gaelic. "It is not with thee we would fight. We remember thy kindness in the days of old, and with thy father and his race peace be all their days, though ye have melted like the snows on the dyke, and have drifted from the preservation of the true sons of Morven by your own misdeeds. Go your way : we have enemies between us and our own hearthstones. Death to the bloody lairds that send the Camerons from their native glens."

Following this speech with a wild brandish of his axe, his followers, some of whom were also armed with such implements as they found ready at their hand, joined in an in-furiated cry for vengeance, and pushed their leader forward upon the path where Alan and Arnot stood, in advance of others, who had now joined them, bewildered for the time by the mad band of peasantry.

"Go back," cried Alan, excited, "you abuse the hospitality of Finzean. It was by my wish that you were asked to partake of it ; I was answerable for your behaviour : will you make me ashamed of what I have done ? Return, I say, and we will discuss your wrongs ; you will bring yourselves by this madness to the jail—maybe to the gallows."

"Curses on him who threatens a Cameron

with the gallows-tree," cried the mad member
of the clan, who now stood forward in defiance
of those who confronted him. Drawing his
body to its full height, and casting the axe
from him with the shout that "a Cameron
never took an advantage," it was the work
of an instant to spring upon Alan, and endeavour by the strength of his long arms to
throw him to the ground, that he might place
his foot upon the supposed calumniator of his
clan. He had the advantage of attack, but
Alan detected his intention in the throwing down of the axe, and met the grip of his
assailant with the full force of his tall and
firm frame. The instantaneous grapple of
the pair permitted no chance of its preven-
tion, or of interference ; and, with bated
breath, both sides looked on, trembling for
the result. It was the hug of two strong men ;
one of them possessing the strength of deli-
rium, which concentrated every nerve and
tissue of his frame, every spark of the vital

being aroused to a fearful energy ; the other, calm in the consciousness and energy of right, and growing stronger as he felt in each movement of the struggle a double call for exertion. The fire of the maniac declined at its first fury. Alan's increased. The pair tossed for a little, a strange wriggling mass beneath the moonlight, the shadows mocking their rivalry. Alan took his assailant in a grasp which revealed no strain, but needed and gathered all the more power, and Cameron lay flat beneath him on the grass. Without a murmur or a cry from either, both rose. No sooner was Alan on his feet than another Highlander, probably the only other of the party who could present himself for the trial, seized Alan, and endeavoured to throw him. A cry arose against the injustice of permitting this second attack thus suddenly, but it had only been made when the assailant was thrown, while Macalpine himself stood straight as a pillar.

"Forgive me, Cameron, if I have offended you," said Alan to the first Highlander, whose hand he now shook.

The fight had sobered the infuriated champion of the peasantry. He muttered his sense of Alan's victory. There was no rancour remaining in him because of his fall. It was no disgrace that he had measured his strength with a chief of the Macalpines and been thrown. But his rage was a little spent, and with the result of his leadership the rage of his followers was cooled. They went back to the barn, where Alan joined them, and remained for a little, hearing their rough jests about the knight, and counselling them as to their plans. Pleasing would it have been to Alan, as to any sympathetic student of character, to have witnessed the change in the demeanour of many of those crofters, as they were permitted, at a late hour in the night, to join their "betters" in the house. How painful is the burning aversion in the human breast to that false and oppressive social superiority which corrodes the natural and healthy craving of man for a true kindliness and equality.

Coming out of the barn to return to the house, Alan met Miss Mar, who had remained evidently behind the others, who, with her, had witnessed the fraternising; she had a long cloak and hood thrown over her, which protected her from the cold, and almost from observation. She was in the way of Alan as he left the door, and in the moonlight, by her partial removal of the hood, he received a full view of her more than commonly animated countenance. It smiled.

The demon of forgetfulness was in Alan; all was buried in present passionate action. The uncertainty of his career, the gibes of his father, the sense of present failures with his lot in life and with his love—deeper chagrin than, a year before, his well-regulated mind could have believed possible—spurred his fagged hopes into a wild wrestle-fit. Here before him stood the aggressor who seemingly had desired to

fced him with what she believed must be the
grandest hopes of his heart, that she might,
with the delicious tyranny of fair woman, dash
these asunder, after she had completed the
severance of his truest love.

"I have observed all you have done," she
said, as she took Alan's arm, and walked slowly
with him, in the brightness of the night, into
the path, which was now clear of shadows.
"You have to-night fulfilled my conception of
the modern hero;" she said, with gaiety, while
Alan was unaware that her heart beat more
rapidly as she uttered the words.

"You are privileged to-night to use the language of romance—the queen of the revels has
but to approve, and not even the object of her
eulogy may detract from it. But may he speak
the language of sobriety towards the majesty
who favours him so liberally, since to claim the
privilege of romance would be impertinent?
Have I your leave to speak?" asked Alan.

"A thousand sentences!"

" By your presence here to-night, you reveal the possession of a nature truer than that of hosts of your sex, who would affect to despise these simple, humble revels."

" Is that all ? " she said, with disappointment manifest in her tone.

" You would not have me deal in the tinsel-ware of unreal compliment; you—who can mea-sure things at their true worth, and probe the pretentious victims of vanity—who have cast aside the dull vacuities of the false livers around you—may listen to plainness of speech."

Alan paused, and changing his tone from elevation to an abrupt lowness, continued : " Come, if we have anything to say to each other, let there be no hyperbole : both of us are equal to facts."

Lucretia Mar felt a slight tremor at this language. She was loving, but dallying. All was pleasure to her, though there might be suspense and a little terror in it.

" You are sudden with your victim," she said ;

" too eager to drag her from her pedestal down
to the cold implacable earth. You play only
at idealities, and when they may yet delight
you throw them away, and take the sharp hard
tools of work in your hand." Her voice was
passion admirably simulated, if it were not
that of passion itself.

Alan started. His own heart beat high.
Victim !

He drew her towards him, going forward past
the house upon the lawn, protected by the tall
trees from the slight south-west wind which had
now risen. The moon was still clear, and seemed
to give heat, as it gave radiance, to all that met
its beams.

"'Time," he said, in a low, sententious manner,
as if he hesitated or paused idly ere he dashed
upon his course, " seems at the outset to permit
for us all many and divers delicious voyages.
It permits, in reality, rather but one, and that
often a poor one. To-night, Miss Mar, I again
find you by my side, attracted by some law in

nature or events ; it must be for the last time, or for all time."

" Why this terrible speed? must we go breathless upon our destiny? is the world so dependent upon our decision that we cannot take pleasure in rambling by the way to it? must we at once eat the fruit, or turn away for ever from it ; and those delicious idlings through a land flowing with milk and honey, be unpermitted as pernicious?" Lucretia Mar inquired, in tones faltering between soft interest and passion.

" You place me on the defensive, but I have not yet completed my part as aggressor," said Alan. "I must repeat that time is short," he continued, with that momentarily dry humour which was to his companion not the least of his attractions. "Remember my second interview with you," he continued ; "your anger at my approach, and dismissal of me—remember our next meeting, your great service to me, and your subsequent avowal—nay, deny it not

—you would have chained me to your side for reasons you will yourself know. But with to-morrow came your change, and with months came obloquy for me. To-night you won-drously seek me out; I ought to have passed you by, but in consequence of that mysterious bond which will not permit us to be apart, I meet you smile for smile. The siren shall not leave me till I disavow the virtue of her charms, or confess their power."

As they walked in elegance for a time, dig-nified but fervid, by the fading influence of the moonlight, Lucretia Mar was able to see the glow of the strange passion of the man's heart. Her own was still really with its pleasures when he began to talk to her of love, and as he went on questioning the meaning of her conduct, the old fear of his force of character stunned her. She had never been dragged to the bar of justice by man or woman. Yet she did not flinch or shake from her heart the clinging in-fluence of this one, who arraigned her now with strong eager questioning. He had acted in the way to win her. "I owe you great reparations," she said. "Colonel Mar has been the cause of my singular conduct. But do not press me to say more now ; I cannot, or I would." She wished him to speak : her own voice was unpleasant to her, and she waited to hear again language which moved the depths of her long cool, unruffled core.

"Then I am to remain ignorant of all save the knowledge of fate's—or rather Colonel Mar's or your own—inconstancy."

"Yes, now you must," she answered, mustering all the boldness she could.

Alan felt that the woman who leant her head upon his shoulder out in the winter night was his at that moment. Far away, miles upon miles of glen and mountain, river and loch, were revealed, which he passionately loved as the inheritance of his fathers and the home of his heart ; now he had but to speak that they might be restored to him free and unencumbered as they had never been for many generations. How few men could, in his situation as he stood, have had the first thought other than the joy of restoration. But Alan was blind to the sight set before him. The pride of his untamed race was far deeper in him than love of soil, and from it sprung some of the nobility and courage of his character. He had been wounded ; he had been wronged ; the wild spirit of justice must have its dues.

"Is it not," Alan said, with slow emphasis which penetrated the core of her whom he addressed, "that your actions have been commonly dictated by the sense of your own needs, rather than by that of justice and sympathy ; that your support and stimulus in your daily life are truly material ? Is not love, as long as this fashion of mind lasts, a mere gay clothing to be set up to toy and dandle with, and to be cast aside with the other idols of the hour ? "

Lucretia Mar felt the knell which was rung for her, as the man who held her gathered

together his sense of her sin, and sounded it
with determined strokes. But there was a
balm to heal the tingling pain of the indignant
rage which came upon her. Did it not appear
that the castigator was also a pleader ; that
while he resented her conduct, he admitted
her power ; and upbraided her cruelty in the
language of one who loved ? She had wished
to withdraw herself from Alan as he attacked
her character. But he held her firmly, and
she was powerless in his arm, which had
already that night shown in another way its
strength.

"How can you hold converse with such a
demon ?" she asked, scarcely indignant at the
strong words used concerning her, while she
confirmed the truth of the observation that
women, as men, are offended rather by the imputation of petty defect than of positive wrong-
doing. "Am I Mephistopheles, the tempter of
the weary, jaded Faust, that you are attracted
to what you revile ? See, there are actual

temptations spread before you ; you are deeply
sensitive to the claim that your native lands
have upon you; become their lord again ; they
are before you, and are yours if you will but
follow me."

This was said in mock, as if the speaker
refused to answer the charges made against
her, and exhibited herself sportively with them.
The indelicacy conveyed in the speech struck
the tenderest chords in the other's frame.

"I treat you," said Alan, "to an accusation from
a high judgment-seat. If I were addressing a
weak woman, I would not be severe. I am jealous
even of your strength. If you have offended
me, shall I not tell you how that came about ?
Of you, Lucretia Mar, who are capable of nobler
thoughts and actions than ever dreamt of in
your own breast, I ask whether I have spoken
truth or a lie."

"It is true that I have done wrong," she
muttered. Her haughty pride was gone, as
she was ushered face to face with the real

meanness of the side of her living presented
to her, and she stood in the touch of a man
whose character she knew to be infinitely noble
beside hers.

Alan did not think now ; he yielded himself
at the confession; and his blood coursed rapidly.
He led Lucretia to a room at the back of the
house, lit up by the remains of a comfortable
fire, which had been used in preparations for
the feast. "Now that my aggression has ended,"
he said, "you may begin your attack." His
eyes were bright with excitement.

"I have none to begin, except to challenge
your severity. What woman but would tremble
to be in the power of such a man. You are
most uncompromising," she answered, familiarly
now.

"But I can be most loving, most candid,
most self-condemnatory. Life would be a sorry
sweetmeat without the character that can con-
demn as well as approve ; it calls out the
flavour of love to try its strength in the fire."

"You estimate your command of it highly," she answered.

" Why do you not then attack me? say that my antecedents and my mental means give me no title to assume the right to speak as I have done, and assert that my continual habitation with inferiors in rank and education has given me an over-estimate of my powers? Why do I not consort with superiors and equals? Is it not because I am too proud to seek my own level? Ah! there may be truth in this ; but I have found a sufficiency in self, amid the high melancholy mountains, the still lochs, the deep world-suggesting forest of my native land. Not now, however, is all this always sufficient. Woman has intruded upon my solitude, and I am vanquished by other charms than those of inanimate nature, and the poet's selfish love."

By the glimmer of the fire Alan's companion saw the change which came over his face as he spoke. The censor had become the poet and the lover, and with the metamorphosis came all the tenderness of the greatest spirits.

Through her own untaught hardness, Lucretia Mar wondered and loved the romantic soul of the man before her. How very far from cruel he was when, the moment following his indignation at the wrong done to him, he revealed the softness of his heart? It really seemed to her that she could have worshipped the image of the poet as he stood before her, with all the fervour of a devotee whose natural craving for some idol to satisfy the heart had been long checked.

A movement was made by Alan as if it seemed he wished to return. A cry of pain was upon his companion's lips. "Not yet," she cried, seizing him with both arms, "we have the privilege of confessional now; after so much brightness and so much storm together, it is painful to move. Tell me, Alan"—she used the Christian name first—" that you forgive me for all the wrong I have done you, and that in my sense of the wrong, and your goodness towards me, I may become such an one as that life will be truer, nobler for me."

The shadow of a woman's figure seemed to fall within the door, which had been left open. It might have been only a shadow, but Alan thought it was the person of a woman that stood for an instant a foot beyond the lintels.

"Come away," said Alan, "we are keeping the people out." They went out together, Lucretia leaning upon his arm. The south-west wind had further risen, and the clear strong night had vanished ; the air was warmer, but the warmth came with a sky overcast with clouds ; the moon was obscured; scarce a star could be seen ; and the wind howled amid the dark leafless trees. It was the break-up of the calm, deep brightness of one of winter's best days. The landscape was no longer visible. The two who returned to the open space looked forth into a dark blank space, where only a little time ago was an expansive territory.

"Faust is not fated," said Alan, with a solemn humour, "to enjoy the land of promise. The gift held out to him a moment since is vanished from sight. There is an augury in this change from light to darkness."

" How can a Macalpine, whose fate pointed him out centuries back as the winner, have so much womanish dread," urged Lucretia quickly, with a feeling which was partly of his humour.

" Where is the bloodshed which thaws with this southern wind," asked Alan, after the same fashion."

" In your own breast," cried Lucretia ; " your heart bled and froze after my attack. It lay cold as this melting ice towards the door of Morven. To-night you have taken me captive ; your heart has thawed ; but ere it did, the daughter of Morven's hand in your own had restored the lands to Macalpine's heir." She was passionate. Alan looked upon the woman who leant upon him with an eager stare.

"Is there no fleeing from the fulfilment of this prophecy," he inquired, softly.

"Never," she cried ; "you have confessed the power of the siren."

Alan said nothing. The gust broke through the trees that rose far into the dark sky above the insignificance of the two mortals who had stood underneath for a minute ere they passed. Its eerie touch struck a chord in Alan's breast. He turned round at Lucretia Mar's last words, and the sweep of the wind smote him at the same time. Again it seemed to him as if the form that had stood but a minute before in the doorway looked down upon him from a knoll above this spot, on the walk which wound down to the front of the house. With the cry of the wind he fancied came the whisper of a human voice saying "Faithless."

"Why do you not speak, Alan ? Your hand grows very cold. You ought to have been provided with covering as I am. Why do you stare there as if you saw something strange

through the darkness ? Let's return within.
In this Highland home we hope to spend many
happy years, when each son of the mountain
side will have his own land and his days complete to him ; they will be the finest people in
all Scotland, and the strath will hold at its head
the name of Macalpine." As she spoke she
covered him partly with her thick capacious
cloak.

"Lucretia," he said, feeling only the woman's expressed tenderness, while the fatal
words escaped his tongue, "I do confess the
power ;" and he kissed the lips which were
so close to him, and his extended arm held
with a keener ease the slight recline of her
fine form.

A few minutes, and Miss Mar, after bidding
a good night to the host and hostess of Finzean
Farm, was driven to Morven Castle. The
sound of the carriage wheels fell in the gusts,
and died away in the distance.

Had he, then, been tempted and fallen ?

Good God !—fallen to the earth, a poor crawling worm, to lick its slime for ever ! Oh ! that he might blot it from his history, and flee the wrath to come ; but there was no returning : time had flown from him for ever, and already registered with implacable hands the indellible fall !

He had buried his head in his hands as he sat, and the cold winter wind beat upon his sides and benumbed his blood. He rose after a while stiff and pained, and returned to the house. His face plainly indicated the recent passions and griefs that passed through his spirit. He reeled as he entered into the warm, noisy, and well filled apartment where the guests were already seated at supper. He might have fallen as he observed the seat reserved for himself occupied by her whose memory he had just stifled. He started back first with a vague, fearful horror that his brain had conceived unearthly images, and then with a pained apprehension he wheeled back into the

open night. Was it a dream ? Away through
the dark woodland and the lonely moor, he
returned home, fleeing from Ellen Lee, and
from himself.

CHAPTER XX.

Awaking early next morning after his adventures at Finzean, Alan found himself in a fever. The events of the preceding night he ran over, incident for incident, word for word, with fatal memory, which increased his fever by the torment of his brain.

It was not love. The confession of the siren's power came at the moment from the heart, but it was the evolution of admiration and of pity alone.

The beauty of her form, the strength and ease of her mind, the splendour of her surroundings, the regaining of a noble inheritance which he had lost, were influences which he felt with full force. But this was not the grand contemplation of the future laden with the choicest sweets of being, in which his manly thoughts had revelled with Ellen Lee. Where was consummated, in a marriage with this woman, his longing after felicity, the union of souls? Was she the one who should respond to his dream, and could refresh a jaded spirit by an understanding tenderness?

When Alan tried to rise he found he could not. He was penetrated to the bone by a malady which utterly prostrated his physical strength.

The drover Donald, Alan's attached servant, was surprised at his master, who was commonly an early riser, not making his appearance among the cattle, which at present demanded most sedulous care. He waited long after the usual time, and after the hour of breakfast (Roderick Macalpine and the domestic servant not knowing whether Alan was in or out), and then he went into Alan's bedroom.

With his aid Alan procured writing materials, and wrote at once a note, as follows :—

"DEAR MISS MAR,—If you have not already forgot what took place between us last night, do so now ; forgive me for the wrong I have done you, as you are forgiven the wrong you did me. I am ill with cold, otherwise I would have seen you myself, though probably it is better to write that I erase the proceedings of last night from my memory, as you must also do. This is needful for the happiness of both. We were deluded by a false glare into venturing upon a course which, to try to follow out, the daylight exhibits to be the wreck of both.

"Yours truly,
"ALAN MACALPINE."

Donald went with this letter, and also for a medical man, the first that Alan had ever need to consult.

By the time he reached Morven Castle, quiet had just been restored, after an unusual bustle there, Colonel Mar and his daughter

having left, upon two hours' notice, for London.
It was about nine o'clock, immediately upon the
receipt of his letters, that Colonel Mar, according to Madge's information, broke into her
mistress's apartment, and told her to prepare
to go with him to London in two hours. His
will was her law, though she feared his wits
had turned by the sudden command for so
long and tedious a journey. "It wasn't long
before she sat down to write a bit note to
a gallant young laird you and I know, Donald.
Here it is, but not for the world tell Mister
Alan of it. She left the scrap just as the
Colonel called her out of her room to speak
to her a second time; but she never, when
she came back, took up pen again, but came
back proud like, and sorrowful like too, as
if she and the Colonel had quarrelled. She
forgot the bit paper; but I treasure it, for it's
the wish o' my heart she may marry the young
laird that played wi' me mony a summer's day,
though he thought naething else than that he

was laird o' the haill country, and I a puir grieve's daughter," gabbled away Madge to Donald, who was able to read, on the thick and gold-edged paper held before him, a few lines written in a bold clear hand, thus :—" My dear Alan, Colonel Mar suddenly calls me with him to London. We leave two hours hence. This deprives me of much anticipated pleasure this week. Instead of finding me here to-day to arrange for the forthcoming 'event,' you will only receive this bare paper, explaining that the bird "——

" She 'd been going on to say something fine," said Madge, slily, to Donald, who was " a smart man."

" Why didna she end it, and let me tak back the bonnie screed ?" inquired Donald.

" The Colonel upset her ; he 's a queer man."

" The love 's no deep that a father's scratch can rub oot," remarked Donald. " Aff to Lunnon without a word to her sweetheart!

queer wark that! Weel, Madge, I 'll no tell the maister."

" Ye must tak' your own way as to that," broke in Madge, who was very anxious that Alan should be told.

" But you 'll no tell anither than me," said Donald, " or you 're no your mistress's friend, or Alan Macalpine's. There 's mony a slip between the cup and the lip ; and I hae heard say on the road here, by them that kent already, the Colonel was aff to Lunnon because he 's a ruined man."

" God forgive ye, Donald, for telling lies," shrieked Madge, who saw her consideration gone, and the mistress she had affection for fallen.

" Ye hae 't as I hceved it," observed the cool, self-possessed Donald.

The doctor had seen Alan before Donald's return. Remedies had been prescribed, and among these the usual one of quiet. Alan, however, had no one to see that these direc- tions were carried out, and Donald walked

into his room without meeting any one. He
tossed uneasily in his bed, and upon his face
a settling sadness seemed to struggle with the
fevered emotion which would rise in his heart.
By mental exertion, while it weakened his
physical energy, he brought himself to some
calmness. After he heard what Donald had
to tell him, he turned his face to the wall.

When the storm of the malady had ceased,
after Alan had lain in bed several days,
he recovered gradually. The poetic temperament bestows many resources for hours of
languor, and heals the flesh thereby as well as
the spirit. Alan had need of all the calmness
he could command. During the week of his
illness, the considerate Donald had spoken as
little to his employer as possible, for he would
have had to tell of daily deaths among his
cattle. Disease had been rife there; and when
Alan was restored to a fair strength, at a
fortnight's end, he found that more than half
his cattle were dead.

The sudden disappearance of Alan from
Finzean surprised Oliver Arnot a little, even
although the unexpected visit of Ellen could
not, considering what had taken place between
them concerning her, but render a meeting
painful. His illness, which Donald communi-
cated the following forenoon, explained satis-
factorily the singularity of his apparent flight;
and the honest farmer flew to render assistance
at the cattle-pens, and beside the bedside of Alan.
Late in the afternoon, when the farmer got
back to Finzean, he found Ellen seated at the
window, gazing with a dreamy melancholy at
the thick sky, sending down lazy flakes of
snow, away towards the quarter from which
he had just come. Ellen, though told that
there was nothing truly serious in Alan's com-
plaint, was moved by a feeling towards her old
lover of which she had had no previous experience. An inexpressible tenderness took the
place of the romantic glow which had, in former days, tinged all her thoughts of Alan. The

conception of Alan's misfortunes—attended only by a father little capable of giving any alleviation to suffering—drew from her tears of yearning. What dull stupidities prevented her ministering to the solace of his disease ?· Here was the man, whose image had been the idol of her thoughts and of her dreams, prostrate, and she sat by like an indifferent onlooker. Was this the result of her spirit of self-sacrifice, that the dearest object of her old love, the worthiest of her—of any woman's devotion, should be left to the mercies of the winds, rather than that she should abate one jot of a stern rule of imagined worldly gospel ? In yesternight's gathering storm she had been witness to Alan's strange devotion to the woman to marry whom all his world pointed out to be necessary and right. Ellen knew, however, it was not love ; she almost knew it meant not marriage.

By heaven ! what did she then expect of Alan ? She, after winning for certain his heart, was now to bid him adieu, and leave him to wander restless unceasingly in those groves where he had found her alone, and where he might perish grasping the semblance of herself. Was Alan's future recollections of her to be only as that pleasing vision of life's young dream which the old people of the world, who are not altogether of the world, love to cherish to the last, and which would lose half its zest if it were not shaded with melancholy?

When her uncle entered the room in which Ellen sat, he noticed the traces of her excitement. He was not to her now as he had been, and she could speak freely of Alan. "How did you find him, uncle?" were her eager words.

She had to take off his heavy coat covered with snow.

"Not that bad; he'll soon be out again," answered Arnot, with an unconcern he mustered for the occasion.

"Have you heard anything of how it was come by?" asked Ellen, with a playful slyness which arose with the good news of Alan's condition.

"No, no! why should I—that is—but the bad cauld night, and the ugly change o' the weather, which he'd too much of, with his fashion o' lookin' after the stars," stumbled the farmer.

"Yes; but it was not to learn astronomy, the people say, that he stood out in the night; it was to make love to the laird's daughter," Ellen continued, with a little sharpness.

However considerately just we may have acted, if we interfere with the supposed pleasure of even the most virtuous, we may be certain to acquire a moderate degree of their dislike. Ellen could not just now feel the tender affection she had of yore for the good farmer her uncle.

"He is, then, carefully secret with the court-ship," said Ellen, in her humour of finding fault. "Had it been the daughter, or the niece, of a farmer, instead of the laird, he'd have carried his gallantry openly, that all the country-side might gossip of it, and he care not a bodle. There was one pair of human eyes that saw him injure the repute of the high lady ; and they saw that he did not love her, thinking little of her, and turned to embrace the howling wind, that accorded more with his own spirit, than the breast of her who is no true woman, or Alan Macalpine had not dared to offer her the husk of his love. He is ashamed of it, ashamed to become a victim to Mammon. No, no! this marriage will not be—he is not himself. If he marries Miss Mar, it will be out of revenge upon the injustice of his fate, sugared over with the thought of compensations in the blessings he may bestow by his restoration to his estates ; not out of love."

So, like a woman, Ellen Lee demolished the fabric woven of her own level reflection by a bit of temper which was nearer the truth. But a minute before she saw, in the slow calmness of her contemplation, Alan a happy man, united to Lucretia Mar, and across whose path

came, as a soft vision, the dream of his old love
for her. Now, as she concluded, she saw a
nobler picture, in the heat of her spirit ; some
particular torch being required, even in the
warmest natures sometimes, to set the spirit
at its truest glow.

"Weel, Ellen," replied Oliver Arnot, mightily
surprised at his niece's energy, and trembling
internally at a castigation which he felt was
being administered to himself, "come what
may, I've no reproaches for you nor me;
we've done right. Youth may live on hill-
berries, but aulder teeth maun hae the fat ox ;
and if Alan Macalpine can get back the big
lands by saying, 'Ay,' where's she that would
hae him say, 'No,' without a penny to offer to
buy saut to his kail ?"

"If a man's sustenance be only out of the
flesh-pot, he is simply a cumberer of the
ground, and unworthy to live," answered
Ellen, with quiet pride.

"You are got proud, Ellen, since ye left

Finzean," said the farmer, who expected that his niece, in her long penitence, would exhibit another temper.

She smiled with sweetness, for a moment, in the midst of her passion.

" You will, I believe, think me jealous, uncle," she said ; " but I am not—have no right to be, now that we have gone from each other. I may speak my mind, though, about the ' ox.' Ah ! The affection of an obscure and despised heart may be infinitely wealthier than all the untold possessions of India—a poor Indian maid richer than Golconda !"

" Yet you 're going there, Ellen, to try and get some o' the filthy lucre," remarked the farmer, after a pretty long pause, in which he had felt a painful inclination to give way to his niece's spirit of self-assertion.

She entered upon some explanation of the reason which had induced her to seek a situation as governess to a family proceeding to India, partly that she might discover the history of her mother there. Her uncle only pressed her to stay and live with him, urging his belief of Alan's engagement with Miss Mar, but she would not consent. He did not yet think it right to narrate what had taken place between himself and Alan in the garden, after the visit of Sir Andrew and Colonel Mar.

The farmer shook his head at the investigation of forgotten stories which Ellen had determined to enter upon. She would uphold her mother's name, though she died in the effort.

Then Oliver Arnot was called out of the room, and Ellen being left to herself, without any opponent to support her spirit by the opposition, gave way, altogether, to the tenderness of her heart; and an hour later in the day, her uncle listened to the plaintive-like sweetness of her voice repeating a song she had given the previous night, whose story told of love's sacrifice. She would be weak no more.

Two months was the full time allotted to Ellen to prepare for her voyage, and she in-

tended passing it at Finzean. The recollections
of her former stay there were again strong
within her; she would not have the scenes of
former brightness made melancholy to her by
the gloomy winter of a discontent. She had her
pain in the effort, envying occasionally, as does
every hurt mind, the still life of unconscious
happiness—the unruffled lily of the valley.
But the consciousness of her dangers, and her
faith in her capacity to meet them with even
a certain gladness of spirit, had elevated her
strength. Nevertheless much of her steady capacity to meet her ill-luck arose in her genial
humours. She was not one of those creatures
who are always lamenting to the Comforter.
"Daily bread" suffices, of this world, in the petition of this unselfish and hardy Scottish flower.

After a month had passed away, and Alan
had been for some days sitting up during the
greater part of the day-time, Ellen went to pay
him a visit; she felt ill with the contending
emotions which her brave resolve brought

forth ; it might cost effort in his presence to preserve her proper attitude, and the force of her mind, which should proclaim the sympathy of friendship alone. She met him with pleasure upon her cheek, the more excited that she perceived the calm glow of his satisfaction at her coming. He was still very thin and pale. She had been pained, at first, by finding herself at the door of Alan's room without seeing any person about. His solitariness alarmed and again smote her with apprehension. She could not, *dared not* repress the growing tenderness she felt for her old lover alone with his misfortunes.

"I could not come before," she said, while a certain consciousness of constraint covered what she meant as frankness; "till you were well," she added, in worse confusion.

It appeared to be a confession of her knowledge of his displeasure at her conduct, and the consequent expediency of her keeping away while he was sick ; but she was for a minute confused, and scarce knew what she meant. To come upon her old lover here, alone in his own house, in this fashion, was a strange experience for her.

"You are going abroad," Alan said, when she had sat down in his room beside the fire. "You are making great sacrifices by this course—your own best chance of happiness; at least your comfort and your uncle's happiness are at stake. When one leaves country and friends behind, to be alone in a distant world, strong calls of self-interest or of a great cause alone demand it."

"Perhaps I have a mission," answered Ellen quickly, her eyes sparkling. Alan smiled. His sincere countenance was lighted up as it had never been since he lay down. He saw into Ellen's heart, and there he knew of some flame that had burned in his own.

"I, too, once believed I had a mission," Alan remarked, quietly, but with a shade of doubt.

"I appreciated it," observed Ellen quickly, without any bitterness, but heartily.

"You did: you thought me an enthusiast whose being warmed only by the conjuring spirit of some lofty ideal, with a heart cold and insensible to common love. If the confession be needed, I am feeling how weakly alive I am to this; feeling more for the sympathy of another kindred spirit, than towards all the missions the grandest soul of aspiration has failed to realise."

She was for the time struck dumb. How she had flown into the lion's mouth! She prayed that some supernal being might open the floor, and let her be swallowed up in the wide space of vacuum.

After a little she was able to mutter, "I hope you will find this—if you have not found it." Alan only looked at Ellen. Both felt how difficult it was to speak in honest plainness in the situation in which they stood to each other. Alan found himself following Ellen when he again spoke.

"Is not this, too, fleeing from the vain attainment of one ideal to the search after another? Were it not better to light at once upon the round solid earth, which may be grasped for at least a sure footing, than to fly with uneasy wings?" asked Alan, wishing Ellen to speak as if she led, while he groped in his misgivings.

"It is better," said Ellen, remembering the scene in the garden on the night of the feast.

"I was not surprised when I heard from Donald of your arrival at Finzean—I knew of it before. I saw you three times on the night of your uncle's Yule : once in an outhouse, at another time on the rockery, and again seated at his table. I confess to you that on all occasions I believed myself to be the victim of a hallucination."

"You did not think that appearances so frequent could be accidental; and you could not believe that they were all designed," remarked Ellen, with a sparkle which was bright.

"No! I thought not that way; imagination had possession of me. I was in wonder as to the reality of what I had seen, and what I heard." Alan repeated the four last words with a slow emphasis, which brought blood into Ellen's cheeks.

"You were not surprised, Ellen, to hear rumours of a forthcoming marriage with Miss Mar?" Alan inquired. He was determined that there should be no secrets on his side now.

"I could not be so," was the reply.

"How?"

"Your attentions to her were forced upon my sight."

"You have not hitherto believed that appearances warrant conclusions,"—bitterly.

"The woman whose lips sealed the loving confessions of Alan Macalpine, I had some cause to believe would become his wife," answered Ellen with a quiet pride in which was no symptom of upbraiding, but only justification.

Alan rose uneasily. Ellen motioned as if to bid him good day, expressing her feeling that this was not a meeting fitted to bring his health back. He said it was just what he needed to that end. In his loneliness, she, of all men or women, possessed the balm to remove the distress of his situation; he had no one but her to whom his mind might be opened.

"Now your eyes are opened to the outrage I can commit; did you not at times reflect, whether, after all, I was not a whining poetaster—dawdling, incapable even of the moving force of the vicious, and therefore unfit for the common roads? That you find me a monster who would steal a woman's heart with the cold embrace of hypocrisy, that I might pocket her gold—how like you the man?" A still, almost fierce glare, stood in the speaker's eyes. "Do you not think me this monster?"

"I do not," she replied, firmly. "It must have been from her that the conduct was prompted."

"How know you that? You cannot think me a woman's slave! True, the advances were made by her, but I beckoned them on. 'How?' you will ask. Out of sickness and retaliation. I was mad with the obstacle on the course I had imagined mine. I burned with offended pride at the insult to my name by the action and words of the very woman who would have inspired me with love for her, while her own heart was safe and retired as the snow-peaks of the mountain; and I have taught her, as she may be taught, with the cold weapon she had intended to use in her victory over me. Now, if she be still as rich, in the gilded saloons of London she pauses to think how she will lead her captive Gael over their floors, emulating the haughty Roman pride when he held the tall northerner at his chariot-wheel."

"Are you sure that the pride is not your

own, and that you fear to marry a woman
richer than yourself, just because you will, in
your own sensibility, live in the presence of a
superiority of a kind?" Ellen keenly inquired.

" No," answered Alan, boldly. "Pride I
have, but if it was of that order simply, I
would divest myself of it. I have given you,
Ellen, what I believe to be the true revela-
tion, and if you think I ought to adhere to
the letter of the contract, say so."

" I entreat you to do so ; you are the victor ;
have mercy towards the vanquished. It
realizes the wish of your friends ; it places
you in a position of power, to command esteem
and goodwill for yourself, and to those just
actions upon which you would base your title
to consideration ; without it, you have to face
neglect and contumely. Where you are tossed
with natural anxieties for the future, and even
shifts for the present, you will be lifted into
a region of peace and plenty, and your intellectual cultivation will proceed unimpeded by

the babblings of trading." She spoke breath-
lessly thoughts thought out to words she never
believed she would use.   Her heart confessed
to itself the suspense, which her mind wrestled
with in all its force.

"Stop!" cried Alan.   "What becomes of
you ?"   He blushed with shame.

She sat still and stiff; the rising blush with
her, too, came, and could not be kept down,
Alan keeping his eyes fixed on the ground ;
and there was silence for a minute and more,
each fixing their attention, in the pain of the
situation, to the tick of the old clock on the
mantelpiece.

"The picture, Ellen, glows garish and unreal.
I cannot complete a fraud.   I wrote Miss Mar
next day cancelling the engagement.   It has no
charms for me, who have known the richer
elements of life.   Is it a curse or a blessing
that my imagination has warmed by the
reality, and not by the show ?   I would be
miserable in the clutches of the latter, and will

be happy only in drinking still of the sweets I have known. 'Miserable babe,' says the man of the world; 'do you not believe that these are the mere dreams of childhood, and that you ought to seek the substantial fruits of manhood?' Well, be it so, I know the value of both; and having known them both, my choice lies with the endeavours to consummate these dreams."

"If you have sought and gained this woman's love, from whatever motive, you are bound to fulfil your contract," said Ellen, quickly, again pushing onward her mind's resolve.

"Her heart is dead to all the pure influences of the noblest passion," cried Alan.

"Time may restore it to some native integrity," observed Ellen, quaintly, humour visible.

"Never! so long as its mainspring is Mammon. Even now, she holds aloof from writing me, till she sees whether she remains a great heiress. There is some mystery about the origin of the advances she made to me. I am not vain enough to suppose they arose from a preference to myself personally; but there is no mystery, I believe, about the cause which may bring these advances suddenly to an end. That morning she left, she had begun a letter to me before she knew the cause of the sudden journey to be taken; when she was made aware of the possibility of her father's ruin, she tossed the letter aside—for poverty to marry poverty would be madness for her. I know this to be true. Colonel Mar told me more than once of a colossal speculation in which he was engaged, which might nigh ruin him, or be his enormous gain. He loves such excitement. For months I may not have an answer to my letter, till it be seen how the scheme ends; if it fails, I will never hear at all—never see the woman who offered me her hand and her gold. Does not that prove to you that this is not love! I am free: the case is proved."

" You will see how she comes to act," Ellen said. She knew fully from the first Alan's amount of self-will.

" Do not think any more of my case, Ellen, think of your own," said Alan, in tones changed to gentleness. " I have spoken plainly of the ill that 's here about my heart; keep not yours quite dark, if I may serve you."

" You cannot serve me, or to you I would come for help. Other dear names are concerned in my mission, and it must be sacred even from your arguments for the present." Ellen evidently feared the thorough sifting mind of her lover. Alan perhaps felt this, saying no more on the subject.

" If you must go, do you return soon ? " he inquired.

" That depends upon my discovery. It is more likely that I may remain for many years," she replied.

" Then you leave us small hope of seeing you again; have you thought that your constitution may be lowered, and its health gone amid the arid jungles?" remarked Alan, with some bitterness.

"It may be so; I regret vastly my going, but it is laid upon me, and I fulfil the call of duty."

Alan could not but smile. How like was this talk of high design to what he would himself have recently used. He could not believe that Ellen was truly justified in what she was about to do. He would have revered her, had he seen her devoting herself to a heroic design. As it was, he knew that the mistress of his heart had her virtues outwith the ideal.

"Are you serious, Ellen," he asked, "in placing your going truly to this mission? To your uncle, who seemed to break his heart on your account, I promised never to see you again, rather than that you should quit Finzean, which is your natural home. You know, Ellen, how I can subdue myself: before you came I renounced all hope of seeing you again,

and I flew from your presence ; and again here
I will renounce all my former hopes of seeing
you again—will ask you to say whether we
meet, or never again, each erased from the
other's memory—that you may remain at
Finzean, and lead the life intended for you.
But I counsel you by the Word of the living
God not to act falsely. Say the word alone
from your honest heart—love or indifference ;
if the fatal breath comes by the pressure of
corruption caught from the world, or grown
up within, you will never know peace again."

There was a force in the last sentence which
recalled to the mind of the hearer the fierce
determination expressed by the speaker on
former occasions, when the latest of the Macalpines exhibited himself to be a man whose
word was inviolable to a degree which invested
it with pain. A minute before she had said, in
answer, that she entreated him to fulfil the
contract with Lucretia Mar. Then, however,
she confessed, neither were speaking out of the

depths of their individuality, but only as the common run of the respectably moral people of the world would do.

The human breast will part slowly even with the forlorn hope ; but woman's love may not let her part with that :—

> " Return with all thy torments here,
> And let me hope, and doubt, and fear ;
> Oh ! rend my heart with every pain,
> But let me, let me love again."

Now Ellen, her love excited, and that partly justified by what she heard, was brought to the irrevocable end. Could she now pronounce the fatal words which should break them two asunder?

Must she declare she could not seek to promote the happiness of the man whose love was hers alone,—possessed of a passion which his strong will would only smite down that she might live in the comfort marked for her ?

"No, I cannot lie. I have not the power to renounce my love. It was given from heaven, and I cannot tear it from the roots and cast it away," was the language of her heart, scarcely upon her lips.

She rose in confusion, not knowing what she said. Alan observed her lips move, and her face bear all the emotions of that tenderness, the depth of which he knew, and he had not a word to utter.

He heard a word or two, and she was gone.

The day was not unkind as Ellen went forth. It was a relaxation from the winter's fury; the sunbeams fell unmolested, the wind only gently moved the beech leaves in their weary hold, and the ground was firm and dry with recent frost, which was kindly in its strength. She walked long, and the sounds of nature soothed her, ere, for the first time since she returned, she dared to take her way alone through the wood towards the little bridge on the stream where she had first met Alan.

Her heart was full all the way with him she had left; she felt she was more bound to him than ever she had been ; that he was more precious to her, as she saw she was more precious to him who had need of her.

She threw herself down on the hardened sod of the stream's brink, beneath the overhanging branches of the dark, grievous-looking pine, but from beneath which she could look into the ethereal sky, while her heart, as her eyes drank of the calm, sought guidance for its troubled course.

CHAPTER XXI.

THE cattle disease had played terrible havoc among the stock of nearly all the farmers of Morven. Only Oliver Arnot's farm, whether, as the neighbours had it, from accident, or by the peculiar ministrations of his wife, was so fortunate as to escape a visitation altogether. More unfortunate than even Alan, because he was not made penniless, the crofters upon Sir Andrew Cameron's estate had their only wealth taken away from them in the death of their cows; insufficiency of food and shelter rendered the poor animals easy victims.

It grieved sorely the hearts of Oliver Arnot and Alan Macalpine to witness the wretchedness of a peasantry fallen from a state of proud clanship and vigorous bodily life. From the time that the owner of the soil came to treat it and its occupiers only according as he might think he was able to increase his gain, while he might reconcile that with a specious public benefit, they dated the decline of these hardy sons of the mountain-side. Arnot, with patriarchal love, cursed the iniquity which had broken down the interdependence of the chiefs and the clansmen ; and asserted that never till their mutual service and affection were restored, would the position of the country's prosperity, in her people's vigour, return. Alan, imbued with all the fervour of the creed of the new age, knew that these relations, however attractive-looking still, were of the past, and no longer possible ; that the age for the all—for the people had arisen. The remedy was not to restore the dependence which should create the meaner affection of lord and master, but to institute independence, with conditions calculated to inspire mutual respect and affection.

While the farmer and Alan were discussing their views, both were engaged in practically affording some assistance to the crofters. Alan would not directly interfere, for to him he felt the recent grudge was yet extended. He knew how long despair makes ill in mind as well as body, and he cherished no anger as against ingratitude. Sir Andrew Cameron, on the other hand, having heard of the wild proceedings of the crofters at the Finzean feast, vowed that he would exact his rights to the uttermost farthing, and warmed his wrath against the day for rent and for removing.

Arnot had written to Colonel Mar, stating what had taken place, and he had now received instructions to administer relief secretly. It was a sorry sight to witness the easy stages by which the remains of once stalwart frames, in the clutches of gaunt poverty, came to extend the mean hands of beggary. Oliver Arnot wept as he turned away from the sight of it in men, some of whom, and all of whose ancestors, had possessed the eagle eye of proud clansmen.

Candlemas day came ; and a deputation of

the crofters waited on Sir Andrew, to represent the state of the case of each of them, and to pay him what they could. He was greatly enraged at their petition, that, considering their losses by the death of their cattle, they should be allowed sufficient means to take them to America; they were condemned as a set of lazy hounds, who ought to have been there long ago, and before they had spent the money he ought to have received as rent. They simply stared at the man : their spirits were broken. What knew the elders of pushing their way in the world? their home had been all the world for them, and in it all their ambition and their love lay. In the owner of the soil, now in the act of pushing them away from it, not one spark of real love of country remained. He was that dead soul who never to himself now said—" This is my own, my native land." They returned to their homes disconsolate and sadder even than they had left, when they bore with them half a hope. The message

they returned with to their wives and families
was, that each cot must part with everything
except one bed and bedding, a wooden chest
and a pot, and that all the proceeds of the sale
of the rest, and all other moneys, must be given
up, except a trifle for conveyance to the nearest
seaport. Unless the money was paid in the
course of eight days, the effects would be sold,
the tenantry sent to prison, and their wives and
families ejected. Thus dealt this head of the
old people of his family glen, in exaction of his
claims. Alan and Oliver Arnot endeavoured to
arouse an interest in the matter on the part of
the farmers and stockowners who had no
occasion to dread Sir Andrew's vengeance on
themselves; and, heading a subscription, a sum
was obtained sufficient to maintain them for a
short time, if it did not suffice, with other
assistance which might soon be procured, to pay
their passages in the ship soon to sail for
Canada from the seaport.

When Ellen was going about the dismantling

of the cottages, or rather hovels, now to be
left to their exacting owner, she could not help
wishing that fate had been kinder, and Alan
and she have associated together in the work
of assisting their unfortunate neighbours.
Tenderly had she touched the thin, weather and
hunger coloured, children, and the cracked, worn,
household effects which were the earthly gods
of the poor crofters, as she felt that sympathy
which makes the sympathiser one with the
sufferer; while she thought that, with the
assistance of a practical man like Alan, she
would be of double use, and enjoy the more the
labour of love. She sat down one morning
by the side of the bleak winter-worn moor, and
pictured to herself Alan and her together in
their expostulation with the evil doer, over-
coming his cruel designs. Her imagination
became excited with her new sense of philanthropy, and in a bolt of determination she
resolved, herself, to set out on the mission of
reconciling the sinner Sir Andrew Cameron

with her sense of right. She thought she was prepared to argue the case with the laird on abstract grounds. Besides her heat of indignation, raised by the scenes of misery to which she had been a witness, she herself had fuel of her own to the fire, in personal cause of quarrel with Sir Andrew. She was not one to brook wrong with mealy forbearance. Sir Andrew, by her outspoken zeal at Mr Jenkins', had been the immediate cause of her leaving. She armed herself upon further reflection by returning to Finzean and getting her little pose of money with her, and with this aid she hoped to have the better of the laird, should her mission of justice fail. She had recently turned the most of her daily thought and attention upon the cause of the crofters, and she now imagined she might by a dexterous stroke even foil the exacting landlord.

It was five miles distant from Finzean, and the time was winter. But the day was fine, the hour was early, and her spirits were high.

Was there anything else that added decision to Ellen's steps towards Sir Andrew's habitation? She had not forgot his looks upon learning in Jenkins' house that she was a niece of Oliver Arnot. She had told her uncle of this: the explanation that they had never been friendly since he returned to this country did not, however, satisfy Ellen. Besides, she learned something of his offers on the occasion of his recent call at Finzean. She imagined there must be something more, and with the readiness of one bearing a mission, she associated Sir Andrew's mysterious emotions with a knowledge of, or connection with, the history of one or both of her parents; and, little as she was given to chimeras, she could not divest herself of the fancy that Sir Andrew, having been in India, could tell her of Dr Lee.

As she arrived at the gate which opened the way to Sir Andrew's house, she sat down to rest and consider finally the plan of her campaign. She looked up at the old massive stone

pillars, upon which swung the rusty wings of
the iron gate : all around was the stillness of
a winter noon, when nature is not in repose, as
in the summer night, but seems dead : man
left alone to himself and to the reflections of
his own fleeting day. How be a restless curse
to his fellow-men in such a suggestive scene!

The coat-of-arms cut out on the pillars took
Ellen's attention. She had seen this design
before. She was sure that in her mother's
house, years ago, when she was young enough
to inquire without receiving any satisfaction,
she had asked her mother concerning a carving
of a picture like to this, which she had observed upon some trinket. It was strange that
this should occur to her now. Were not such
crests common to many families? Yes ; but
considering the suspicions she had brought
with her, was not this an additional fact,
pointing to their being well grounded ? Ellen
took out the cameo brooch she wore at her
neck, and held it in her hands. It had been

her mother's. The figure appeared to be that of Apollo, the back was of plain gold, and not massive. It had seemed to her that the brooch was heavier than the material warranted. She thought of pressing open the back. It was not a work of great difficulty. The gold back, she saw, had concealed another of massive make, with embossed work, upon which Ellen's eyes now rested with a strange apprehension. Her face flushed deep red in the cold air, as she gazed upon the design. She did not replace the false back, but put the whole in her pocket, and walked slowly, with an anxious countenance, towards the knight's mansion.

Sir Andrew and his nephew were together when Ellen was ushered into the laird's breakfast-room. With that puffed and offended look which a pompous man puts on when he is intruded on by an unwelcome inferior, he received Ellen. "What was it?" "Very busy," and such like, were the mutterings which greeted her. Treatment of this kind brought Ellen to a state of mind fitted to attack. But her grand abstract arguments somehow vanished from her mind.

Ellen said that she wished to settle as to the rent due by four of the poorest of the crofters whom she named ; that she would pay one-half now, and the balance a year hence.

" Where have you got this money ? " asked the knight, angrily, throwing discredit upon what he gathered to be an eccentric generosity. " ' The earth is the Lord's, and the fulness thereof,' say they who take other people's money," he cried.

Ellen looked as if she fell in the presence of the icy heart of the old man.

" What security will I have that the other half will be paid," he added.

" I am young and in health, and God may preserve it for a year in India, where I now go; and my salary will soon enable me to remit you the amount. If you refuse my offer, not a penny of these rents you will receive," answered Ellen.

" Whew ! " whistled the knight. "You knew, probably, what the scoundrels intended for me when your worthy uncle had made them drunk. I must decline your proposal."

" I entreat you to accept the money, and let these poor people go," cried Ellen.

" No, no ; you must be off ; I can bear your interference no longer." He thought her a foolish young woman ; but he began to suspect some device by which a laugh would be raised against him. The knight was most sensitive to the lash of laughter.

" I offer you the money, then ; it will go hard with you to put them in prison now. You dare not do it after this." She counted out the bank notes.

She had picked up the information from her uncle that imprisonment was not competent for a debt under £8, 6s. 8d., which was more than the balance due by each crofter after crediting the payment she now offered.

The knight could not conceal his rage. He felt the possibility of being outwitted.

"'Gad, don't refuse money," urged the Captain, who did not see so far.

"Curse them and their meddling friends. The rascals must go to jail; and they that have aided and abetted them, let them look to themselves. I may have my foot on the necks of some of them yet."

The knight moved forward, as if to show Ellen the door.

She now thought to startle him. "Is there no power which may move you, Sir Andrew? See here; will the memory of times which this recalls soften your heart to my prayer?" and she set close to his eyes the brooch which she drew from her pocket.

It was an embossed crest and motto, with his own initials beneath.

He looked with eager eyes at the article presented to him, though without betraying surprise. He whispered to Captain Hamilton to leave the room for a little. When he had gone, he simply asked Ellen where she had got it. She explained. "Far from softening me, girl, the sight of that brooch might harden me to stone. It reminds me of my own weakness— of tender kindness requited with treachery —of the vanity of believing in such a thing as gratitude. Sit you down and hear the story of your mother's shame."

She sat down mechanically ; her strength taken away for the time in the dreadful surprise and suspense. She had gone about her investigation, as she had been led to it, with abrupt strangeness, and she was answered similarly.

"You expected," he continued, "to receive from me a denial of the knowledge of this article. I believe I may trust you with some disagreeable truths which concern myself, but may put at rest odd fancies which you may have got through gossips. This was the second present of jewellery I gave your mother. I sent it to her from abroad, with a letter inviting her to come to me there, that we might be married, as it would be years until I could fulfil in Scotland the promise which I had made. It was long quietly understood I was to marry her ; her mother, the only woman in this earth who I ever found of the right sort to the end of her days, wished the marriage scarcely less than her father, who insisted on it. I would have married no woman except your grandmother's daughter; and they knew it. I was to marry her and give her a grand outset, because I was a grateful man, a finer man than an idle brainless rascal, with a 'blether' of fine words. It was an excellent match for her, but she had not sense sufficient to carry her through. When I got to the vessel which landed her on the Indian shore she was "——

"Married! to whom? tell me that, Sir Andrew, as you value your peace in earth, and hopes of heaven—speak to me the truth of God," Ellen cried, as he stopped and turned aside.

"I let them have their own way," he muttered, occupied with his own passion.

"Did you never inquire, never learn who had married my mother?"

"It was your own father, girl: Dr Lee."

"I thank Heaven that was so. I never knew of my mother's engagement with you, sir; if it be as you say, she had cause for grief; many a time have I seen her weep over the past, which was a sealed book to me; there must have been strong reasons to influence so good a woman to turn away from her obligation."

"You are thankful there is nothing worse than this, I daresay," growled the knight. "From what you said now, you had imagined your mother was married to another man before Dr Lee."

"I had my fears, but they were very vague; though I knew that Dr Lee had not been alone the suitor for my mother's hand."

" Well, bury your fears now, and forget all about them."

" Thanks, thanks ; oh, a world of gratitude for your assurance. You have proofs of this ? Your own knowledge will be sufficient. I must make all clear and plain to the world, which has spoken such harsh words against my mother. You will assist me, Sir Andrew," she implored, with simple-mindedness. Sir Andrew thought this was not a cunning woman. The knowledge did not improve him.

" No, no, not I; not a bit of assistance. This is all you get. Moreover, you must not speak of what I have told you to a human being. I will not have my name mixed up with it in any shape. I am not disposed to have the whole parish speaking about my private con-cerns. Keep your tongue to yourself. You may have a cool hundred or two from me some day."

There was a glow in Ellen's heart. She smiled at the knight's airy generosity of the future.

" I thank you, Sir Andrew," she answered, at the door, " for these good intentions, as well as for this information ; but it will be better that there be no gifts passing between us."

" Then I 'll just save my notes."

"I would you could bestow them on those that have need of them." She was a pleader again.

" I 'll throw them in the water, sooner than feast ungrateful dogs."

"You are ungenerous, Sir Andrew ; but perhaps you have some cause to think badly of your fellows ; so may I have," and she looked in the face of the knight with such archness that he started back. "You re-member," she said, with this humour visible, " how you got me sent away from Mrs Jenkins."

As she passed along away from him into the passage which led to the door, he stood looking at her with an irresolute anxiety, in which pain had the predominance, while a tinge of light seemed struggling within the obdurate

constitution of the man. But he turned
quickly on his heel after a few minutes, as if
surprised at the thought which might have
struck him, and he was soon immersed in
those schemings from which the pleasure of
his days was got ; somehow or other, however,
after a little he became restless and uneasy, as
if some ever-recurring thought which had pain-
fully seized possession of him would not leave
him. He looked out upon the distant prospect,
and calmly as he endeavoured to realize in his
imagination the secure designs at which he
aimed, the sense of a new difficulty struck him
with dispeace.

When Captain Hamilton returned, the laird
impressed upon his nephew the desirability of
his departure for London, that he might again
offer for the hand of Lucretia Mar, immediately
upon his learning of the safe landing of her
father off the shoals upon which his speculation
had got him. He no longer believed that
Colonel Mar would have any other heir than

her. He would give the Captain access to
quarters where information bearing upon these
points would be readily obtained. And he
must go to London himself; he had some
private business to transact which required immediate attention. The nephew was surprised.
Knowing, however, that matters were serious,
as well as secret, which laid such a call upon
his uncle, he at once consented.

Sir Andrew managed to fall asleep that night,
but he awoke with a start immediately afterwards. Plainly the easy-minded gentleman
was sadly disturbed. He rose and lighted his
candle, and in dressing-gown and slippers trod
the long and cold way which brought him to
the room, on the floor of the house, which con-
tained the store of his papers. He had managed to curb his mind of its restlessness in the
daytime without the solace which seemed
stowed in this region; but the old man could
no longer shut out the strange uneasiness, and
he knew now he could not sleep till he satis-

fied a craving of his eyes. He knocked about two or three charter chests till he got a key, with which he again opened a strong oaken cabinet. There he seized from a bundle of papers the original deed of entail under which he succeeded to his uncle's estate, which document he unfolded, and scanned eagerly. He threw it back with disappointment, although he had known the terms of the deed, almost word for word, from the hour of his succession. Then he entered another department of the cabinet in which a small bundle of papers lay, and he counted them. They gave at least by their presence there satisfaction. He returned to bed and soon fell asleep, the old man's brain quieted for the time by the physical and mental exercise he had undergone.

Next morning he was not the man he had been. He felt no longer in the sun ; and the ripening fruit which he was growing seemed to shrivel up.

As for Ellen, she slept soundly enough

over her encounter with Sir Andrew, and the story he told her. It was simply nothing more to her mind than that he had been a rejected suitor for her mother's hand. But she was pleased that night, and for many nights to come, with the assurance, such as it was, that Sir Andrew gave her.

Reflection afterwards face to face with the most momentous action of her life, again awakened all her old fears that her mother had broken, under the impulse of an ardent love, the moral law of God.

CHAPTER XXII.

On the first day of the month of March, no change had taken place in the movements or relations of parties. Colonel Mar and his daughter had not returned from England; Sir Andrew Cameron and Captain Hamilton were also still there. Ellen was yet at Finzean, the wife of the gentleman who had engaged her to go out to India having taken ill, and the voyage been postponed. The crofters were not yet evicted from their dwellings; Sir Andrew having given no instructions, and being known to be occupied with other pressing concerns, the delay was set down to that cause.

No longer surprised that he did not hear from Lucretia Mar, Alan ceased as much as he could to think of her. Her silence under

the circumstances he knew she was in, bore
no other reflection than that which had occurred to him the day she left for London—
she was bound up altogether in the accident
of fortune, and had tacitly acquiesced in the
resolution announced by Alan. Not a word
came from Colonel Mar or from any other
person, to tell how his affair was speeding, but
in jeopardy his fortunes were very well known
to be : it was the chief talk of the county.

That Alan had not yet heard from Miss
Mar, was known to Oliver Arnot, who could
not conceal the fact from his niece, Ellen, as he
would have done had his temper not been
roused.

"There looks nae muckle love in this,"
muttered the rather enraged farmer, as he
knew, from what Alan told him, that the latter
had not yet heard from her, who all about
considered to be his betrothed.

"Contradict these rumours, Arnot, wherever
you hear them," Alan had said sharply several

times during the last two months ; "they were at the beginning as ill-founded as they are now." Alan told his friend frankly what had taken place between him and Miss Mar ; to Arnot and Ellen alone he confided the result of their encounters. "Our acquaintance," said Alan to the farmer, "is now over; I have written to her twice without an answer : henceforth I know her not. It was an idle fancy favoured by my father and you. I was brought into a relation to become the sport and creature of a woman with whom I had nothing in common. My pride received a shock, and I became for an hour a character which my sense of my wrongs obscured the evil nature of ; the result is shame to me and now to her, and we are both punished. I pray only that it may be forgotten."

It was at this time that Alan began to plan the putting in order the cottage which his father and himself were to occupy at the next term. He had been so impoverished by his father's loss of the remnant of his mother's funds, and by the death of most of his stock of cattle, that he found he would be unable to keep the Lodge which they at present occupied. With him it was beginning the world again ; and it would take a few years, at least, to form a capital upon which he could enter the market and make his trade yield the return to which he considered his skill entitled him to look to. The rent of the cottage, which had been at one time occupied by his father's forester, was much less. There were few rooms in it ; yet Alan felt there was no real injury to his comfort to be faced. The cottages of which this was one, which had been erected under the solicitation and care of his mother, were substantial, roomy, and dry, and were, moreover, in situations where the eye and fancy might receive pleasure in the surrounding scenery. Edith Macalpine acted towards her people as she would have acted in planning for herself. Those pure delights of which she was herself cognisant were

just those which, in the simplicity of her heart,
therein wiser than "men of understanding,"
she imagined were cared for by others; and in
so estimating the feelings of others, she acted,
unconsciously, in the very way to bring into
existence what really before had being only in
her imagination. Alan felt his father and himself were now to reap the benefit of his
mother's benevolence.

The cottage was built at the confine of a
luxuriant wood, upon the south side of the
river. It stood alone, looking from a high pro-
montory far up in the glen, over river, meadow,
and cultivated fields, to the blue misty mountain tops, which receded farther and farther.

The refreshing breath of spring had come
over the sharpening region of Morven that day
that Allan visited the cottage. It was even a
day when the ground, still bare and forbidding
otherwise, shook off its chill, and responded to
the rays which lived in the air and sparkled
upon the water, penetrating the sombre green

woods, the voices of whose inhabitants burst through their sickliness. Alan sat down, and for the first time for many months, that religious emotion, full and strong, which comes over health in moments of calm gladness, suffused his heart.

A commonly sensitive man of the world, in Alan's situation, would either have been broken down with despair, or have aroused himself to some desperate work by which he might hope to regain steps lost. Alan's paternal estates were gone ; he, a man of education and of old ancestry, became a dealer in cattle, and was no longer inquired after in the social circle to which he was born. But he was content and happy—happy as the temper which Providence had assigned to him would permit him to be in any circumstances. He had had enough of means, even beyond common necessity. But now he was reduced further in the scale, so that every farmer around him, if educated to reckon consequence according to worldly

estate, would treat him as a poor inferior ; and
he was now deprived, for a time at all events,
of the complete means of carrying out intellectual and other employments from which he
derived enjoyment, and might also derive commercial profit. But he felt to-day full content
and happiness ; poverty not actually staring
his father and himself in the face. Chill
penury had ne'er repressed his noble rage, nor
frozen the genial current of his soul. Every
man, Alan thought now, of moderate material
means, can gratify a love for nature, and for the
choicest records of human thought and imagination, and may recreate in the common socialities.
And what needs he beyond to enliven the ruts,
or give tone to the sweet places, of labour ?
It was the philosophy of the life he thought
he was come to. He turned upon the records
of other lives, in history and fancy, in whose
presence he loved in hours of ease to dwell.

It was already an hour past noon on this
sunny first of March, when Alan still lay sur-

veying his future home and its surroundings, that the voice of song broke upon his ear, and aroused him into listening. It was a cultivated female voice, and it being a rare circumstance to hear song of any kind issue from these woods, as this did, and especially at such a season, he was amazed. It was a Jacobite air, expressive of parting sorrow for a beloved Prince; plaintive, yet full of spirit. Alan rose,—yet why disturb her emotion or his own pleased fancy ?—and he threw himself down again on the bank, waiting eagerly upon more expression of the soothing voice.

> "That strain again, that strain repeat !
> Alas, it is not now so sweet !
> 'Twas suited to my passive mood,
> 'Twas hopeless love's delicious food !"

It was Ellen Lee. She charmed the wood with her notes as she had of old him,—alone, she breathing to the listless air, while he lay aside, to her no more than a stone of the valley. Alan rose again; between him and

the wood lay the river, or, ere time for reflection, he would have penetrated the thicket; it
was easy enough to run a few yards up and he
had the bridge, but in the time he thought of his
obligation. He reseated himself again, after his
restless movement and dumb eager questioning
of the wood. The singer had ceased, if she had
not flown to other regions.

She had come along through the woods in
the fine March morning, intending to pass
over the bridge at the northern side, to make
a call at a farm; and, on her way, to see the
cottage to which Alan had to betake himself.
When she came along, she saw he was there
before her, and hurried back the path she had
come, fluttered with the coincidence of her
interest and his concern being manifested at
the same moment ; and blushing in the dark
wood like her younger self, as if it were
renewing first fresh thoughts of the antici-
pation of conquest. After an hour she returned
to get over the bridge to the roadway, which

she required to do, or to go round a great
distance.   Upon her errand to the cottage
being accomplished, she sat down and chased
a rising melancholy thought away with the
song which Alan had heard.   Rising, and
coming nearer to the water, she saw Alan
lying upon the bank of the stream, she herself
being quite unobserved.   Ellen eagerly watched
for one minute Alan's moving expression as he
lay in the sun.   Every bright hope, every
shadow, which, perhaps, she rather imagined,
passing over his countenance, excited similar
emotions in her own breast.

Events had now come to pass which opened
up the way for Ellen confessing herself.   She
had held out long, and she could hold out no
more.   There, beneath the dark lowly spread
boughs of the pine, she mused with beating
heart over its final succumb to the love and to
the power of him who lay unseeing, watching
only the passionless stream that passed his
future home, and with whose calmness his

own breast then accorded. It was with a proud gratification that she thought to make such a man happier, and to call off the melancholy of his passion for inanimate nature. Nor did her woman's pride fail to pass over in lively force the fact that Lucretia Mar's rivalry was vanquished. Ellen had known, felt with a keen instinct, her rival's mean estimate of her power; though that had never, beyond a moment, moved her to a jealous pang. She thought now only of her services. Her lover, for whose misfortunes she mourned, had need of her. He was poorer than when she knew him first; he was not able to provide for service as formerly, and she had been taught to work at all the employments of a domestic household.

As Ellen saw she could not get over the bridge without meeting Alan face to face, she returned by the pathway in the wood. To run upon him deliberately was a step for which she had not sufficient boldness; for she could not go forward to him, and shake hands, and say, "Forgive me, Alan, I have been in the wrong ; take my hand for ever."

While she walked along the shaded pathway, a reaction followed her terribly serious though satisfying mood of the last hour, in which had been concentrated the thoughts of two years; and she made merry with the words which would remain in her fancy, "Forgive me, Alan ;" take my hand for ever." She pictured to herself her extended hand, borne with the cool assurance of a despot princess towards a favoured lover. How surprised would Alan, with his earnest character, be at an easy advance like this? Ellen stood and laughed and laughed again at the fanciful picture which had taken possession of her. Once Alan and she had so stood and laughed together, as they tossed to each other the description of a ridiculous adventure. She remembered the occasion now with double force, until the trees seemed to nod with the merry peals of responsive laughter.

It was very evident that there was a load taken from her breast. Alan was not very far behind, and heard what was going on now. It was his turn to observe, and round a corner of the pathway he saw Ellen holding her sides. Was his Ophelia mad?

Ellen had evidently, in her interest in his fortunes, visited the cottage; what great gaiety of spirit could arise at once upon the sight of that, save of some change caused thereby in her own emotions towards him. " Her gentle and free spirit sees one for whom her cup of love is full, because it is less and less interfered with by the materials which destroyed it in her fancy; her heart is buoyant," cried Alan.

Truly Ellen's spirits could not be repressed; she walked fast, and then slow, singing, sometimes humming some favourite Scotch air. She was not now far from the Falloch Bridge, where Alan and she first met. He wondered what she would do when there; that is, if she

could do anything else than merely walk over.
Quite loudly she sang now. The words of
the song, "Oh! whistle an' I'll come to ye
my lad," were clearly heard in the stillness of
the thickly-clad wood :—

> "Tho' father and mither an' a' should gae mad,
> Oh ! whistle an' I'll come to ye my lad.
> But warily tent when ye come to court me,
> Aye vow an' protest that ye carena for me,
> An' whiles ye may lightly my beauty a wee ;
> But court na anither, tho' jokin' ye be,
> For fear that she wile your fancy frae me."

Alan kept back until Ellen had finished.
Then, without a moment's pause, he whistled
the air of "Handsome Nell." He knew Ellen's
familiarity with the words of the song beginning :—

> " Oh ! once I loved a bonnie lass,
> Ay, and I love her still ;"

and, as she knew, the first performance of
Burns, and, in his own words, "the spontane-
ous language of the heart," when it "glowed
with honest warm simplicity."

She knew it was Alan who whistled behind her, but she dared not look back; she was at the bridge and she walked on it, but when at the middle stood still; somehow she stuck fast and could proceed no farther: there was Alan almost at her side standing on the bank. She blushed deeply, and attempted to hide her confusion by speaking first, turning to Alan, saying, " I have forgot myself, I "——

" But not me, Ellen. You must come to me now; have I not whistled long enough? Remember our first meeting here: I went with you, to-day you come with me." He led her back with his arm tenderly upon her.

Around was not that bright open splendour of scene into which nature had burst when they met here before; already the sun was being obscured in the heavens; yet it was a day of promise, an earnest of the opening spring in which all the world rejoices. Both instinctively turned back in their thoughts to the delicious moments in which they first knew each other, when the charms of earth and sky vied with their own enthusiast hearts to cast a seemingly everlasting halo of delight around their lives.

"We have both met with some rude blows since our first meeting here," observed Alan.

"They have given me strength," she answered.

"We shall rest upon our earliest recollection," he answered.

"You must think me a strange being," Ellen said, still trembling, so that Alan felt her shake in his hands. The whole force of her uprightness—the strength with which she had reined her emotion during these years—had gone, and she stood now beside the man she loved as the flower to be gathered by the hand for which it grew.

"A fairy of the dell, such as I would have had you, when I saw you first?" Alan inquired, wishing to restore Ellen to her mirth.

" Rather the wild woman of the woods,"
she answered, with more composure.

" The wilder the better ; it will accord
with the life led here : you are just beginning
to forget the proprieties learned in the town,
which turn some men and women, particularly
the latter, into mummies," Alan rejoined.
" You will complete, Ellen, what you have
begun ; we shall enjoy the use of all our
faculties—sing, dance, laugh, and joke with
every power you possess."

" I am prepared for harder work," she
answered, firmly.

" You come to simplicity, Ellen ; so far I
believe you will, as you expect, be all the
happier. In the summer up with the lark ;
enjoying the freshness of morning, the mind
wanes to a soothed sense of completeness as
the sun sinks in the west. You will have
charge of the cottage, which will occupy you
during the middle of the day, and in the
morning and afternoon, the produce of the

little farm will have your attention. In the evening we will have music, and the social gatherings will neither be few nor without animation—there are yet old residents of the glens provided with mental volumes of story and rhyme, and history, concerning those regions and their people, which will fill your imagination, in odd times, with new emotions. Oh! it will be grand in every season; nothing now can separate us," and Alan sealed with a kiss the bond which they had made inviolate before God, and was to be made before man.

With a completeness, which never avoided every material consideration, Alan told Ellen everything concerning his pecuniary affairs; how he had lost almost all his means, how he had taken the cottage at the other end of the wood, with the small farm called Ben Alpine, on the other side of the stream, which he meant to cultivate; and that he had no fears for want of sufficient money wherewith to support her and his father and himself, especially seeing the acknowledged excellence of his skill in the cattle trade, which he could not fail to exercise to some advantage.

"Not long ago, Ellen," said Alan, "I would have done injustice to your brave spirit, and have spoken in the cold language of prudence because I am now poor, but to estimate a true woman is to find a treasury ; we have no need of the bank."

They had now reached the bridge, from which Alan observed that the horses and implements for which he had waited had arrived at their destination, which enabled him to commence some operations on the ground, preparatory to laying in the seed. Ellen hesitated as Alan was about to lead her to the field. With an imploring look she turned to him, which he discerned to be the expression of the tenderness of the grown woman, fearful to take the leap in which her heart delighted, while it and her mind were reluctant as they thought of others. Nevertheless, both were gay, and

Ellen had given way ere she permitted Alan to laugh lightly at her fears.

> "Look thou but sweet,
> And I am proof against their enmity."

And she repeated the soft reminder of Romeo's mistress, when he presumed upon his stolen knowledge of her consent.

> "I should have been more strange, I must confess,
> But that thou overheard'st ere I was 'ware."

"It is not rash, nor unadvised, nor sudden," answered Alan, reversing the language of the Capulet.

"But it was tacked to my self-confession that you should warily tent," said Ellen.

"I have been ashamed," Alan observed, with a stern composure for the moment, "of another relationship; but in this one, I glory."

Ellen was touched with a sense of the wrong she had done Alan in her speech, already related, that afternoon her uncle had returned from Alan's bed-side. The zeal with which he uttered in her ear the words, "but in this one, I glory," told her how cruelly in error she had been in imagining that in Alan's open courtship he was least considerate of justice.

The delight with which Ellen viewed the fields composing the little farm in which she was to become a sharer, was very great. The green weedy grasses, which were already appearing on the soil, possessed an interest not unpleasing. The turf dikes, the present dilapidated palings, which enclosed and separated the fields, were dearer to her, by far, than the most solid wall of a baron's castle. She drank out of a clear spring which trickled outwards from a nook at the end of a field of natural grass, and bathed her face and hands in the pool. How delicious it was to her! Never before had water seemed so precious. And when she saw Alan yoke the horses to the plough, and send the coulter deep into the earth, and speed it onwards by the fresh and willing team—an operation she had never seen

Alan at before—she laughed merrily at the
sight, as if she were entering upon a life of
new activity and delights, and had reached her
element at last; laughing because she had no
other way to express her sense of happiness,
while she pretended to criticise Alan's plough-
manship, knowing that he had not so worked
since he learned in his boyhood.

They parted after some time, when Alan
had returned to the foot of the field close to
the road; and as Ellen took her way, on her
intended visit, he rested for five minutes upon
the shafts of his plough, and watched the lithe
figure go down between the long natural
arbour of trees which covered the sloping
ground towards the west.   The last of the
day's sunlight struggled through the leaden
sky, and struck the scene with a golden hue
for two or three minutes; and Alan was full
in his heart with a gladness such as he never
before experienced.   Ere Ellen was lost from
view she turned round, and seeing Alan look

her way, she let her handkerchief stream in the breeze, and laughed again, so that Alan heard her voice till she was out of sight, while he, following her in her gay demonstrativeness, with his bonnet hit the air even for some time after she was gone. He felt a freer man than he had been for years.

Ah, to the closer love of this sweet heart because of the simplicity, let a snowy pillow of Finzean that night witness, as her eye melted with joy!

In simple child-like faith—of wisdom, not of foolishness—was this last of the wooing won.

CHAPTER XXIII.

NEITHER Alan nor Ellen revealed at once the engagement they had formed : yet it was only three nights following that delightful hour passed together, after the meeting at Falloch Bridge, that the fact was out. Out of compliment, farmers occasionally give assistance to a neighbour, and no sooner was it known that Alan had commenced operations at Benalpine farm, than several of them agreed to complete the work of preparing the ground for the seed. This they soon effected ; and so pleased was Walter Malcolm, one of the Ballatruim tenantry, with the exercise of a spirit of generosity and of goodwill towards a Macalpine, generally regarded as no friend of his landlord's, that, with further enthusiasm, he found himself the entertainer at supper of about forty guests the same night. Ellen and her uncle were there, as was Alan himself. Malcolm was pleased with Alan's forbearance in the matter of the attack at the church.

Alan's conduct had given rise to much gossip within the last few days ; about which the irrepressible lady of Finzean opened up immediately upon her entrance into the presence of the host. " What needs he, Maister Malcolm, wi' that bit scart o' grund, that ruined Robbie Allan. It 's got a lot o' stuff laid on 'ts back syne his day, but Alan Macalpine, wi' a' power o' turnin' manure oot o' whin busses, 'll mak' little o 't; he 's a bonnie judge o' a stot, an' gin he mak' the hillside fatten their banes, he 'll turn the tables on ye a', for makin the groat gae the length o' the saxpenny bit. Oh, but this is a wee bit play, Maister Malcolm ; some stour i' th' een o' the gossips. That fine lady, Miss Lucretia, comes doun frae London this week, and Maister Alan's the young laird o'

Morven in a couple o' weeks after. Dinna tell
me there 's something wrang—naething 'll gae
wrang wi' yon lass, or wi' ony man that comes
beside her. Maister Alan kens, like ither fouk,
whaur the gear is, and the auld Macalpine
lands."

Oliver Arnot, seeing Alan make his appearance in the room with his niece, felt apprehensive that the beliefs of his wife were but ill-
founded, and his excitement made him cry
out to "Mistress Jess" to "stop her tongue."
She was beginning to expostulate with this
crustiness of temper, when the farmer suddenly rose and whispered at her ear, "I wish
what ye say may be a' true ; but look there,
are not Ellen and Maister Alan mair to each
other than they were three nights back ?"
This placed a damper upon the exuberant
spirits of the farmer's wife ; she did little
but silently scowl upon the knot of the
younger members of the party, standing at
the other end of the room, of whom the pair her

attention was called to formed the conspicuous centre.

Alan's dress seemed to Ellen to correspond more now with his settlement as a farmer; and it appeared that she also had caught something of the style of the true agriculturist, redolent with the freshness imparted of the sweet air and the green pastures, and gay in the frank humours of freedom. The sense of their choice of a position in life which afforded labour and independence, and the happiness of their joint devotion, rendered both cheerful without alloy.

The young laird, as he was sometimes called after he was so no longer, had always been a favourite with the younger farmers, and since his determination to remain in the neighbourhood and join their ranks, even in a humbler way than some of them, their esteem and affection had been increased. This kindliness of feeling arose chiefly from his personal qualities, which made him a young man they liked to meet, and caused him to be respected, combined with the educational attainments he was represented to possess throwing a lustre on their ranks. His frankness with the class had hitherto suffered because of the uncertainty of his own life. In his situation he could not but in a sense "dwell apart ;" now that he had taken a farm of his own and a wife among them, the community of his spirit grew more familiarly. The farmers partly felt this ; though doubtful if yet to be the comrades of their former laird. But the ruddy cheeks and the blythe eyes and the warm thick work-stained hands moved with animated glow and wild gesture in that group which now welcomed Alan as a settled "tiller of the ground." ·He was in the vein of the occasion, was native and to the manner born.

The group of talkers, in which Alan had been given the centre, stood aside to admit the approach of an old bent figure of a man, who, dressed with an old-fashioned but superb neatness, and wearing in his attenuated counten-

ance an eager and impressive eye, was regarded with interest by every one who marked
his presence. He was a tenant next to
Malcolm's farm, and had been a martyr to
rheumatism for many years to such an extent,
that he was rarely beyond his own doors. His
disease, however, had rather increased than
diminished his interest in events imperial and
local ; and though Alan never remembered to
have seen the old man, he had heard frequently
of him, while the latter himself frequently
referred to the son of auld Macalpine, to those
neighbours who visited the cripple, to chat
over the news, and listen to the keen, and often
bitter, criticisms of a Tory of the old times.
Creeping sideways, with a smile over his
withered face, which indicated the curiosity of
one who doubted, but had sufficient strength
of mind to credit, if satisfied, an elevated
character, he took hold of the hand of Alan,
and shook it with a warmth which he only
qualified by a slight shake of his bent head—

meant to express humorously his disagree-
ment with Alan's professed principles. This
was the signal for a lively, but not over loud,
laugh on the part of those who noticed what
took place : they readily appreciated its meaning.

"I have seen your grandfather, sir," said
the old farmer. "I drove my father to vote
for him at the last election he contested—a
brave man, and had many enemies, for he was
aye in contest where there was honour at the
stake. After the day was lost I was hurrahing,
being a mere laddie—not thinking the joy was
for his opponent—and the laird hits me on the
head, kindly enough for all : 'Jock,' he says,
'aye mind wha ye are;' and I have minded
that to this day."

"Well," answered Alan, heartily smiling, "I
hope I will be as resolute in sticking to my
colours as my ancestors were to theirs."

Such are the varied compositions in human
nature, that had Alan, upon his family fall,

preserved a prudent and not over-done demeanour of superciliousness to every inhabit-
ant about, and have exercised the distant
tyranny, in some way, which ancestry might
have been supposed to have bequeathed to
him, there were not wanting those who
would have regarded him on such account
with respect and honour.

" I welcome you here, Master Alan Macalpine," continued the tart Tory ; " but I am
sorry to do so too. I would have wished to
have seen you Laird of Morven and Member of
Parliament, as your grandfather should have
been before you."

" And so he may be," interposed Malcolm,
who now joined the group, " Sir Edward
Sinclair is dead."

With Sir Edward Sinclair's death it was
supposed that a Whig would now have the
best hope of success. After a " pleminary
cheer," as the host denominated a slight re-
freshment in strong liquid peculiar to the

mountainous regions, and suited to its cold
and bracing air, the party adjourned to
another apartment, which had been cleared for
dancing and blind-man's-buff, while the elders
might be accommodated elsewhere with cards,
and an earlier introduction to the substantial
entertainment of the night.

When the party sat down to supper, the
conversation turned upon Sir Andrew Cameron
and his crofters. The old Tory, who had
attacked Alan as to his forgetfulness of his
consistency to family position, asserted that
they had been imprudent, and were much to
blame for their present misfortune.

"No sooner," said he, "do they pree a pretty
mow than they must have a marriage and half
a dozen weans before they're well buckled.
Deil a one of them ever thought beyond the
morn's morning, and if they sow their kail-
yard with one week's potfulls, they'd think not
twice of pulling the whole for one day's grab."

Alan admitted the carelessness of many of

these people, but contended that there was excuse for losing heart. They were ground down ; with better treatment no happier people need be. "There is a people," he continued, " too prudent to be happy, who have abandoned the simple tracks of life, to fight for artificial refinement, and their natures are wrecked. There is a prudence which may be equally selfish, and more debasing, than the careless imprudence of these crofters."

"Well, sir, and what would you have ? " cried the old Tory tenant, looking up straight, in his excitement to pose Alan.

"Two fat sheep from yonder lot in the Willow Glen for food for the poorest of the crofters," Alan answered, with blunt humour, which gave no offence. The company was rich with laughter. The old man's voice was not heard amid the cries of " Agreed, agreed," on the part of the host and his other guests. It was understood that the sheep were to be provided. A demur was now heard coming from

another guest—apprehensive that he was next,
being a bachelor, and somewhat given to extra
economy, to be called upon to contribute to the
support fund, "That men should not reap where
they had not sown."

"But if they have had no chance of sowing,"
cried Alan, the recognised champion of the de-
pressed.

"What have you and I to do with them?"
cried the man, much for the sake of argument.

"Our ancestry," said Alan, "has made fat
upon them and such as them. The nation has
strengthened and fattened by their predecessors
and themselves. You won't starve the soil,
but the human life may starve. The inheritor
of humanity demands access to the fruits of
the world, which were spread for the reasonable
enjoyment of each. He must work; but it will
not do to say, 'There is no work now,' and you,
the holder of the fruits, to push him away to
poverty. It is the duty of the State (and of all
men composing it, aiding.) to provide, and

watch, the machinery for all who deserve
having a fair and reasonable share of the needful benefits of existence."

To the amazement of the host and guests,
up started, with more erect form than most of
those present had ever witnessed, the withered
possessor of the fat sheep, who had delighted in
his wild wrangle with Alan, not without a pang
at his sudden discomfiture, now wishing to
combine the further airing of his almost forgotten voice and his retaliation. With a droll
waggery which carried along with it the for-
giveness of Walter Malcolm, the host, whose
privilege it was to propose the toast of the
evening, "The Health and Prosperity of Alan
Macalpine in his New Sphere," the little man
explained how he had taken upon himself the
obligation. "I am not often out in the world,"
he said, his voice shaking with weakness and
emotion ; "but I have dragged myself these
two hundred yards, to our friend Walter's,
chiefly to shake hands with the son of the

Macalpines, and to see with my own eyes how
changed that world is from what it was when
I moved in it,—since the grandson of Kenneth
Macalpine chooses to hold the plough instead
of the sword, and sets the crofter-man on an
equality with the lords of the land.   I rejoice
not in change," continued the obdurate Tory,
" and I tremble for the results to our beloved
land, when I see the chiefs, its natural protectors, arming men, though unconsciously,
with dissatisfaction."   (Here the most part of
the company groaned, and cried, " No, no ! ")
" Our ancestors fought at Flodden and at
Culloden, but their descendants have forgot
the old ties which bound lord and vassal,
friend and chief.   Now, the bonds grown in
glory, cemented in battle and dangers, and
long held together in amity and mutual services, are burst asunder for ever.   Would that
a Macalpine might have done, so that he
would help to restore these broken unions,
rather than to break them down further.   Oh,

there is yet hope!" with a sparkle of waggery in his excited eye, " I drink, and ask you to drink, the health and prosperity of Alan Macalpine, and his speedy restoration to Morven ; and, with that, come all the family and political ties which such a restoration must induce. Rumour has already announced the event as certain ; and, when it arrives, all we shall ask of that noble property, in the division of the spoil among the less fortunate sons of the land, will be a good many couples of fat sheep, from other quarters than the Willow Glen, to feast us on the restoration day."

With some other remarks the old man sat down. Alan appreciated the knocks which his opponent had given him, as uttered in all truthful conviction of feeling, and he acknowledged the piquancy with which the joke had been turned against him. Out of consideration for him, the company was suppressing its sense of the advantage which the old Tory was seizing for himself, following him by his undis-

guised manner,—part serious, part half in waggery,—with easy understanding. But Alan
led the way in recognition of the appreciation
of the attack which had been made upon him.

After the merry-like buzzing had subsided,
he rose : his countenance changed from the
smile it wore, upon the other's attack, to one of
earnestness. What he said regarding his con-
version to principles which were antagonistic
to those used by his ancestors, and most, if not
all, of the people around him, was neither
long nor new. They were, he said, neither
selfish nor erratic, but had grown with his
growth ; and his early impressions had been
ratified by the increased sense of justice which
was generally, but perhaps erroneously, supposed to go forward with years. His friend had
admitted his own incapacity to judge the necessities of men's minds by modern events, in his
acknowledgment of his retirement from the
world. The relations of men towards each
other had changed. While man must ever

remain social, and honourably dependent upon
his fellows, it was now impossible and altogether undesirable that any man should lean
upon others, with the meanness of childhood,
for the birthright of the common elements
of existence. With a sense of independence
and dignity conferred upon and retained by
every deserving creature, a nobler national
life would arise, to which the splendour of
vassalage was as the glitter of artificial light
to the clearness of summer day. "I have no
prospect," Alan continued, "of again occupying
the Castle of Morven. Rumour, destitute of
truth, has extensively assigned the event to an
early day ; but, should I ever be restored to
the lands of my fathers by the accident of
events—which, however, seems as likely as that
I should be King of Scotland—be assured that
I will regard my succession as simply a trust,
by which I am empowered, while I live myself,
to observe that all justly entitled may have a
fair share of the means of rendering their

existence enjoyable and profitable to themselves, as others. But why promise the spoil of what will never be mine? The event of which a broad hint has been given—a marriage with the daughter of its present owner—could not have brought about the accomplishment of the wish,—the lands would not have been mine to deal with. But my intended wife sits by my side : I come among you to-night a farmer, and I hope to marry a farmer's niece ere another moon has come and gone."

The effect of this announcement was to suspend for a little the breathing of several present. Most of the company believed that Alan Macalpine had in his power the hand and fortune of the daughter of Colonel Mar. For him to throw away such a prize seemed to them little short of madness. The full beauty of Lucretia Mar was much more to their taste than the truth and depth of Ellen Lee's. Had the heiress been old and ugly, most could have sympathised with Alan ; not so when they remembered the magnificence of her person, and the grandeur of her address. There was silence and disappointment as Alan sat down. Not one single heart in the company loved or respected him the more for the sacrifice, except Oliver Arnot, who wept internally with mixed feelings of pride, joy, and trepidation. As the evening had progressed, and the whisper gone round that Lucretia Mar had that afternoon come back to fix the wedding day with Alan Macalpine, each and all had acquired that gratified sense (which the Gael and the Saxon are equally born and bred to), arising in the presence of rank; and the decided announcement that the object of their silent homage remained a " mere farmer " after all, bereft them of the emotion.

Alan saw and felt this. How he could have seized the hand of a man who rose superior to all material considerations, and possessed within him that stuff which set him above the "ignorant present!"

Under the influence of this sense of pride, Alan rose from the seat which he had just resumed to attend to a gentleman who, it was intimated, awaited him for an instant in an adjoining room.   It was Colonel Mar.

Alan had no knowledge of his arrival, or of his daughter's, and he felt on the instant uneasy in the presence of the father of a woman whose relations with himself, while seeming to him like some strange mysterious dream, might to her be matter of very different viewing.

The Colonel was highly excited. " Balla-truim has just been with me," he said, after some preliminary greeting, " and he tells me the member for the Burghs is just dead, and that a Liberal only can get in.   To-night you will ride fast to —— and engage the Whig agent and his staff at double the former fees, and set the whole machinery for catching the electors in motion, commencing your canvass next forenoon.   Don't forget promises of what

you will do for them all. You must win;
then hurrah for St Stephen's."

The sketch of the vulgar way of winning
what, well won and honourably, is the topmost
height of many a high ambition, struck his
imagination with a shrinking distaste, which
overcame for the moment his astonishment.
Alan Macalpine was a man to walk sternly,
even in the face of death, to his duty; he
failed to follow the false beacons of ambition
which lure common men. This, then, was
that first move for the intended son-in-law.
He thanked heaven he was free. "This is
kind and flattering, Colonel," Alan answered,
quietly, "to think of me for such a dignity;
but I have no title to look to it; I must refuse
your generous proposal."

Colonel Mar cried, "Are you mad? I have
reckoned you to be a young man of ability
who should rise in the world with the necessary means; and yet, when I offer you these—
as, of course, I do to an unlimited extent—you

spurn them. This does not surely arise from
a love of inglorious ease, or your professions
are hollow."

" Neither madness nor indolence," answered
Alan, "forbid my acceptance of your offer.
The object, in my case, in accepting it, could
only be to serve a personal ambition for the
acquisition of wealth, of rank, of distinction
in society. None of these are essential to
my happiness."

Colonel Mar remained silent while Alan,
with his arm leaning upon the mantelpiece,
delivered himself of this confession of unbe-
lief in what the world most prizes. The father
of Lucretia Mar was a prey to conflicting
emotions.

" Seek neither rank nor wealth—if you
spurn, young man, what the greatest of the
earth have not been proof against," said the
Colonel; "but seek employment, seek the
natural outlet for your strong views of what
may be done for your fellow-men. You have

deserved my offer. Come, there is surely pride and affectation of cynicism at the bottom of this distaste for action."

"I have decided, Colonel Mar," was all Alan's reply. "I thank you for the great confidence displayed in your offer, but I decline it." He took the Colonel's hand in his, and shaking it with respect and kindness, bade his rejected benefactor good-bye.

When Alan left, the Colonel threw himself back in his chair, confounded by the unexpected and unequivocal negative to his generous offer. "'Tis very strange, 'tis very strange; marvellously so," he muttered to himself. "The youth is wild and singularly difficult to bring down. 'Tis true, 'tis pity, and pity 'tis, 'tis true—this intolerance of the common ambitions. I could not curse; for it was mine until the fatal hour when the demon of a frightful retaliation seized my soul, which has only yet rebounded upon myself. This broken frame, these withered hands—how like a spectre's: because I have gone the road of a frenzied man—forbid me cursing him ; for would to Heaven I too had held to the mind of my youth, and spoken boldly, as he has done ; then would salvation with thee, Edith, have been my portion, instead of the dead possession of riches which I cannot enjoy, and a daughter"——

Tears stood in the eyes of the worn votary of passion, and crawling to the bell, he summoned his servant to lead the way to his carriage, and returned flat and stale to Morven.

CHAPTER XXIV.

On leaving Walter Malcolm's, the unmistakable scowl of Mrs Arnot, who thus avowed her enmity, warned Alan off. Her face was wicked as he had never before seen it. It required the influence of the bright starry heaven, exciting his own deep elated sense of joyousness, to dispel the cloud which the virago had cast upon his spirit. He walked slowly along in that early spring night, looking above and around, far as his eyes could reach, on the slope of the silent hills, suffused with the never-failing charm of nature, and busy with hopes for the coming day.

Alan went partly by a nearer way, over a drove-road, a road in use for driving cattle, which had been for many years a source of contention between the proprietors of Balla-truim and Morven. It was a near cut to Balla-

truim House from Morven; and a laird of
Morven having claimed a servitude over it,
there was much tough fighting in the Law
Courts before the claim was substantiated. As
he came along, he observed a figure at a little
distance, making slow, unsteady progress. The
unsteady pedestrian no sooner observed the
other occupant of the road, than he drew himself up, and took a step or two with the stiff
and over-erect gesture of one who insists upon
his sobriety, flourishing at the same time a
heavy cudgel which he carried, as if to give
warning against any attack on his person.
Alan advanced, and his eyes met the scowling
countenance of Ballatruim. The latter at once
recognised Alan, who imagined he saw in
the other's stagger rather the careless stride of
an angry or rebuffed man, whose potations had
only increased his ill-humour. The laird's eyes
were steady but savage in their stare, and were
evidently under other corruption than that of
over-indulgence in strong liquor.

Alan was to pass him without a word. He had good cause for believing himself to be the aggrieved of the two, yet he had left the laird alone : not, therefore, expecting any real sense of shame on the part of the man himself, or the opprobrium of the county upon a laird of his wealth and influence ; but, a proud man, he would not retaliate upon a vain and a foolish one. Ballatruim possessed for Macalpine all the jealous and hateful pangs of a bad and passionate temper, compelled to acknowledge of the other a superiority in person or prowess : above all, the preference accorded to Macalpine by the new lord and the heiress of Morven, moved him to a hatred deep and savage, such as all the ancestral feud about territory never equalled.

To-night the Laird had learned the Colonel's intention of supporting, for the seat in Parliament, the man he had hitherto sneered at as a rival in his overtures for the hand of Lucretia Mar. Here were dispelled his own chief hopes.

With a heart full of foul and deliberate curse, he frowned upon the calm features of Macalpine. The wish that rose in his brain was to destroy, by one stroke of the weapon that he clutched, the beauty of the face of the man that stood in the way of the gratification of his lusts.

"Fellow, what do you here?" asked Balla-truim, struggling to reach the calm which he saw the other felt. "Have you not lost your beggarly servitude with the rest?"

"I was not aware Ballatruim exacted the law of trespass upon waste ground : if so, all I can do is to return as I came."

So saying, Alan turned and walked fast towards the public road, which lay about half a mile off. He disliked fighting, and he saw that the laird, who was right in point of strict law, was disposed to seize some advantage, which the situation gave him, in laying cause of quarrel.

The laird was not, however, done; he ran forward with his cudgel erect in both hands.

Macalpine turned about as Ballatruim was close upon him.

"Do you wish to speak with me further?" Alan inquired. "There are disagreeable memories which make that undesirable; and it may be well for both of us to keep clear of each other's society."

"You threaten me, fellow," blustered the laird, while he raised his stick without the courage to strike then : he read in the attitude of his companion a strength which made his nerves shake.

Losing his wits, he rambled forth with a pretended drunkenness upon matter which fed his hate, and was intended as insult.

"One word, and I hope the last with you," said Alan. "Be careful. I have hitherto let you alone; but if you do not behave yourself more like a gentleman, I will have you punished."

Turning on his heel, Alan went forward at a quick pace. With mutterings of "coward," the other stood irresolute for half a minute. Sobered as he came to be, the conduct and language of Macalpine, in their further proof of absolute disdain, were the sorest affront which his pride could meet with.

He ran forward to Alan with a firmer, faster step. "Who do you take me for?" he cried, with surer speech; "that *you* pretend to treat me like a hind: I come of as proud a stock as even the Macalpines. We have had the ability to keep our place as gentlemen— not to be kicked to the rabbles' lot, and hug the scum. But I'll deal with you by the old blood; and if the credit I give you for a drop of it be right, you'll give me satisfaction."

Macalpine felt a rebuke of his own disdainful language; had the last sentence of the laird been real, he had risen superior to himself: it was only cunning. Alan did not feel at ease in the thought of any compliance with the demands of the foolish laird. He was unarmed; and there was no ground for the attack, as he was the aggrieved party. To set too deliberately to wrestle and strike with a man heated with wine in a lonely path, would be demeaning and foolish in the extreme. He hoped to get the other off by suggesting, as people do to a drunken man, that the business could wait till to-morrow.

But Ballatruim was not to be put off here. He entered upon a full and seemingly frank detail of how they might fight a duel near Ballatruim. "You've been making democrats of my tenants, damn you; come, knock up one who'll be your second—he'll do this much by a leader of the people." Now, Ballatruim knew Macalpine to be a simple-minded man; while Macalpine saw through and through him. He felt now that Ballatruim, presuming upon his own greater cunning, prepared some trap by which he hoped to involve his antagonist to fatal injury or ruin. Alan believed the man was at heart a coward, who would flee from the

maintenance of honour, where real danger was
at hand, although he would greatly find quarrel in a straw where it was at a distance.

They had walked on meanwhile abreast,
Alan having made no answer to the laird's
last speech, and they now approached the place
where their roads diverged. Alan resolved not
to give way to the irregular demand of his
companion, standing for an instant to shake
him off.

"You are unwilling to meet me, coward," the
laird growled into the other's ear, while Alan
was again brought to a stand.

"I will not risk my life at *your* command.
But the challenge, even if just, can wait till
to-morrow."

"I am beneath resentment, like a dog, am I ?
Can you suppose I can crawl homeward this
night, without biting, like a spiritless cur ?
Aha ! I am not what you take me for. Curse
you, what brings you to my farmers, making
Radicals of them"—swearing and springing at

Macalpine's throat in his mad rage. But the latter stood aside.

"I fear you," said Allan ; "I do not believe you have a spirit of fair play."

"What is your play, double-cursed, insinuating your creed among my people!"

"I will tell you how I fear you," answered Macalpine, while he stood closely face to face with his companion, and looked as if he would have written his words for ever on the face of the man he addressed. Heaven is kind, which does not register each criminal thought and deed upon the front set to the world. "You are a coward at the core, and bear there all the baseness and treachery of such a character," he cried.

Four vile words were shrieked by the other into the midnight air.

The fascination of an over-awing power held the ear of the wounded man to the lips of the accuser.

"I have known you from a boy to take the mean and crooked way to the end you courted :

in the management of your tenantry ; in your
affairs of what you named love ; in the politics
and social life of the county. Remember by
what cunning strokes you ousted the old
farmer of Monzie. Did you keep faith with
Mary Sutherland, when you won her affec-
tions ? What principles had you in the leap
from a Tory to an ultra Liberal ? You took
me by the arm one day, in the hope that
thus you would purchase a few votes; and the
next you endeavoured to wound—nay, perhaps kill—me, in the attempt to recover favour
with the party you had left, and in whose
presence you felt the trembling of the coward,
unsupported in your turnings by the steady
convictions of the mind. I have no faith in
you ; without honour, I believe you to scheme
to entrap me."

"If you do not come I will follow you to
hell," cried Ballatruim, livid between rage and
terror, at a denunciation which boiled in his
brain. He raised the weapon he had with an

adroit backward movement, and brought it over the forepart of Macalpine's head. Fortunately Alan was not altogether off his guard, and had time to move a little, and the stroke fell on his chest instead of his face ; but he staggered and stood speechless for want of breath, leaning on the paling beside which he had been struck.

Not knowing to what extent he had injured Macalpine, his assailant stood for a minute still. The cowardly rascal communed with himself as to whether he would strike another blow over the face ; he approached Alan with stick extended from the point, intending to strike with the heavy nob at the top. No human eye was on them to register the acts; and the vain, foolish, devilish hope was in his heart, that could he now vanquish and maim this man, he could make a fine story of prowess, and Lucretia Mar be got to attend to his overtures.

The rest which Alan obtained enabled him to regain the action of the heart and lungs ;

and as he saw his assailant approach, he was able to draw himself slowly up, so as to give these fuller play. Manœuvring with somewhat of the weapon of cunning used by the other, he pretended still to use his hands in leaning on the paling, while in reality the right one was open and ready to meet the weapon he observed extended for him.

With a swing such as might have been deadly in its effect, the savage brought his weapon to bear upon the face of Macalpine; but with the alertness of a trained hand, the other seized the cudgel with a strong grasp beneath the nob, and by a jerk drew it to himself and threw it away. Gathering up his diabolical hate into his long and powerful arms, Ballatruim leapt upon the partly reclining form of Macalpine. He was received with an embrace he far from expected—one that Alan had successfully practised but lately on the crofters. The man fell like a log among the stones. Alan bent down over his body.

"Monster," cried the victor, "what horror did you intend for me?"

He looked hard and fierce into the face of the man below him. The burning spirit of indignation which was easily aroused in his breast was terribly afire.

There was a dull sullen expression in the face of the laird, and his body lay still. No cry for mercy escaped his lips, neither did he curse with savage desperation the conqueror. It seemed to Macalpine that the man was under the dominion of the worst of passions—self-hate. The fumes of the drink he had had added fuel to his torment, and promoted the death-like tone of his heart.

The heavy rumbling noise of carts at a little distance coming his way penetrated his ears, and brought him to a sense of his situation. The pride of family or rank is never extinguished in a man, however meanly he may be found in his soul rating his own character, and the prostrate Laird of Ballatruim was aroused to fear for the name he bore, were he discovered as he was. He arose cold, stiff, and weak, and with the fear of an internal injury, so cruelly cut did he feel in his side. Scrambling over the paling into the wood to rest himself out of sight, he fell down with a thud upon the other side. Blood came up his throat in quantities as he rose, and he knew his very life was in danger. All was forgotten except the weakness which brought him face to face with the painful realities of the signs of the dissolution of life; and he staggered along in half-frantic efforts to meet with his fellow-creatures, whom he had a moment before been afraid should cast eyes upon him.

Instead of getting out as he entered, in his flight he got deeper into the wood, though close to the edge of the road. He thought he saw, a few steps forward, a broken edge where there was no paling, and he pushed on to it through the brushwood, his eyes dim with the dull distracting weight of fear which covered the darkness of his remorse, and careless, even in the anxiety with which his heart was stricken. The night had grown dark, the moon having been obscured for some time before he had risen from his cold couch, and he failed to remember that the gravel pit stretched some distance into the wood from the roadside. It was to this place that he hastened, after the hurried minute in which he was attacked by agony of fear. He hastened to his death. He fell a great way down in the pit.

Farm labourers, driving their carts from Ballatruim thus early towards the coal pits many miles away, to supply the mansion and offices of the Laird, whistled a shrill pibroch in sheer sense of life as they passed the gravel pit, where he for whom they worked, in their simple, monotonous, but not cheerless, toil, gasped forth a cry for help. It was not heard.

To this lone, lone bed, came to die one who had scoffed at his fellows in their honest zeal, and had treated simple-heartedness with perfidy. Not at once rests the closing veil of death over the prostrate form.

In a few hurried minutes, that face—indicative more recently of evil passions, but which, in earlier times, was not without the beams of a self-satisfied and occasionally good-humoured joy—might it not have told, through all the evidences of pain, down in the miserable pit, of hope as well as of remorse and struggle?

Do they not become mere phantoms of salvation — these beautiful maxims of divine truth—when seized trying to pass by a leap beyond ourselves in the struggle to the future?

But a bloodless old farmer, a broken-hearted and withered young woman, were the first appalling effigies which barred the vision of the prostrate laird.

END OF VOL. II.

PRINTED BY BALLANTYNE AND COMPANY
EDINBURGH AND LONDON

www.ingramcontent.com/pod-product-compliance
Lightning Source LLC
Chambersburg PA
CBHW030640030726
47497CB00006B/1871